Pot.dot.com

Tales of a Retired Outlaw

Crash Taylor

First published by Artfarm Publishing 2022

ISBN 978-0-578-98624-1

First Edition

The characters and events portrayed in this book are fictitious. Any similarity to real persons, living or dead, is coincidental and not intended by the author.

tonya hudson clinton
creative direction

Printed in the United States

Introduction

I was recruited by a secret organization right out of high school.

In the middle of the 1980s, America was losing its dominance in invention and the global supply of information, products and services. There was also a lack of interest in computing technology outside of the business mainframe market. By 1986, stocks of chip manufacturers were down and investors were getting weary. Japanese chips and circuits were making headway into the U.S. market and manufacturing was disappearing

This organization had the foresight to see the functional and market potential of smaller computing devices and a network that would connect computers in homes and businesses worldwide. Such systems were already in place at large universities and financial institutions, but access was limited and few homes had computers. Thinking the market would be extremely lucrative and beneficial to the American economy, they desired to find and focus capital into this industry and weren't afraid to use unorthodox means.

The source of capital would be the California marijuana fields. Marijuana was a huge market and, although most of the product was from outside the U.S., domestically it was the fourth largest cash crop. California was known to produce some of the strongest and sweetest pot available, and if this flow of money could be tapped and focused, large amounts of investment capital could be accrued.

The idea was fabricated in the mid-'80s by a few brokers, bankers, politicians, dealers and hipsters, all of whom seemed to be connected through radical student groups from the '60s, both liberal and conservative. Neatly conceived, the plan awaited proper timing to be initiated. The stock market crash of October 19, 1987, provided the impetus to put the plan into action.

I attended the Bronx High School of Science in New York City, whose student body was regularly canvassed by Ivy League universities as well as governmental and non-governmental agencies seeking the promising minds of the future. Because of the challenging entrance exam, the students who were most prepared to gain acceptance came from private schools. To me, the rich kids presented a robust market. They loved to party and had the money to pay for it, so it was a no-brainer to find a way to supply them. Drawing from all the boroughs of New York City, the student body made up an elaborate network that covered all of the neighborhoods of the city. Any connection we found could be exploited to a greater extent than could occur at a school that only drew students from its vicinity, and this reach extended to colleges via older siblings, alumni, and extended connections.

I grew up near Washington Square Park, which during the '80s was a free-for-all of the drug trade. Every kind of drug imaginable was sold under the eyes of a disinterested police force. There was one section called Psychedelic Alley, which was always populated by a few longhairs selling 'shrooms' and doses. There was an adjacent area where the Yippies sold marijuana while sitting in the grass playing bongos and guitars. I quickly discovered I could buy acid at school and supply the hippies of Psychedelic Alley and turn a good profit, with which I would then buy weed from the Yippies and sell it at school for a further profit. I got a few lucky breaks and worked my way up the chain and was soon selling to the major dealers in the park and to dealers at many East Coast colleges.

Most of what I sold was from south of the border. 'Mex'

was low potency but fresh and green and arrived in large quantities. It came in bales of fifteen to thirty-five pounds and cost around a thousand dollars per pound. My mark-up was small, but demand was so high that I had to schedule customers throughout the week to avoid a line at my door.

During the '80s we started seeing marijuana of much higher potency arriving in New York. Weed grown in California, Hawaii and later indoor-grown from Seattle, began appearing in small quantities. I was only able to get five to ten pounds of this stronger bud at a time and it developed into a connoisseur's market. Most of it arrived through the mail, directly from Humboldt County or Maui to my door. At the time the price was between fifteen and 25 hundred per pound, and even though it tasted a lot better and was a lot stronger, it took a few years for the market for 'kind bud' to build up. By 1986 a stable market had developed for the kind bud among connoisseurs and the market was growing rapidly.

In my junior year I was approached by a woman named Rose, who seemed to know a lot about me. I don't know how she had learned all that she knew, but she was hip to my family life, grades at school and my business. Rose had been a major pot dealer in Greenwich Village since the '70s. She introduced herself at a party and took me into her confidence and became my mentor, arranging my first trip to California to trim weed, my first arrest for civil disobedience, my first menage a trois, a trip to Honduras to help the refugees escaping the U.S. war on Nicaragua, turned me onto Buddhism, Dylan, Sartre—the list goes on.

It was during my fourth trip out to California in 1987 when I found myself in the center of an audacious plan that involved moving thousands of pounds of California weed and a grand plan to finance a revolution in human communication.

Chapter One

I was sitting at a large table with a dozen other trimmers when Rose arrived. We were in the mountains of Northern California at the house of a grower named Little Bear, who grew a couple of hundred pounds every year. It was early in the morning and the delicious California sunshine poured through the large windows that looked over the valley. The table was covered with beautiful, crystal-covered buds and the air was filled with the sweet, syrupy aroma of outdoor weed. We had been at it for a couple of hours already and the remains of a half dozen joints filled the large seashell that served as an ashtray. The wall was lined with garbage bags of plants awaiting our attention.

Little Bear had hired people from all over the country to sit around his table and manicure his crop. We were part of an underground migrant workforce that appeared in Northern California each year to work and smoke the year's harvest. There was a fair amount of secrecy involved in the work and you could only get a job working as a trimmigrant if you came with a recommendation from someone the grower trusted. Most people used fake names, including the growers, and trimmers were often blindfolded when driven out to the farms. The growers were careful as they might have twenty different trimmers work for them each year, which meant that over the years a lot of people could end up knowing where the farms were if precautions weren't taken.

Rose had referred me and a few of the other people I was working with that year. Her word was gold. She had a knack of being able to see someone's true nature and could tell if they were discreet enough and had the required temperament for such work. We worked twelve hours a day, seven days a week, and it was easy to get on each other's nerves. Anyone with a good sense of humor was always welcome. The pay was good and it was possible for a person to make $20,000 to $25,000 in one harvest working ten to twelve weeks.

It was a surprise to see Rose. I thought she was in New York, as she hadn't mentioned anything about making a trip out this year. She was old friends with Little Bear and he seemed excited to see her. She came into the room and picked up a particularly nice bud and held it to her nose. Rose was not a smoker, but she was an astute critic and seemed pleased with the year's product. She said hello to those of us she knew and introduced herself to the rest. She had an easy air, and always managed to put people at ease in her presence. Her disarming smile and inviting personality led one to like her right away. She came around behind me, placed her hands on my shoulders and rested her breasts on my head. I saw a wave of jealousy pass over Little Bear's face when he recognized our intimacy and I wondered if they had been lovers.

I had a good buzz going. Smoking pot since the early morning and having already had a few Samuel Smith's Nut Brown Ales, I was feeling good. The California sunshine and the mountain air compounded the feeling of euphoria that was coursing through my veins. When Rose pressed her flesh into my head, I was so turned on that I wanted to take her right there. I would have been happy to have an audience. Rose had first seduced me when I was eighteen and had taught me to be her ideal lover. She said she was training me for the women in my life. She showed me how to hold off my release all day and how to please her in all the ways she liked. I felt the warmth of her body and my consciousness was filled with the subtle scent of her perfume. I would have been proud to show off her sex and my ability to please her.

She asked Little Bear if he would mind if she took me to lunch and, his infatuation making it impossible for him to say no, we left. As we walked to the door she asked if I minded driving and handed me her keys. We got outside and she pointed to a gray Jaguar XJ-6. She tossed me a smile and said it was her West Coast car. We jumped in and headed down the mountain toward town.

Garberville is a little town that has become wealthy because of the marijuana grown in the surrounding mountains. The local garden store was a thriving enterprise that sold as much fertilizer as some of the biggest firms. The difference was that they sold organic fertilizer in fifty-pound bags, not petrol-based products by the truckload. The town also had a few restaurants and stores that serviced the local community. There was a lot of cash being grown around town, but you didn't see it much.

"Listen," Rose said as we drove down the narrow mountain road, "I want you to be in on my next move. It is going to be big." It was a beautiful drive and she had my attention. "I want to start bringing a lot of this California grass back to New York. There isn't much of a supply on the East Coast and I think the market is ready for it. I am working on a plan that can make us some serious money and have a positive social impact." Rose always talked about social impact. She saw everything she did impacting the whole planet. She was a staunch proponent of the "Think globally, act locally" mindset. I wasn't sure how selling California weed in New York would make a difference in society, but I often didn't immediately understand her perspective.

"We are going to a meeting where you will meet a few more growers. There is an idea germinating. I think you will want to be in it from the ground floor. I think it could be really good for you." She had earned the right; she was definitely responsible for my success to a large degree, but I had things going on for myself. I was young and making a ton of money and I wasn't sure I needed to stay with my mentor anymore. I also had a nice scene and knew that whatever she had in mind would increase the level of risk I was taking. I figured I would go along and see what developed, partly out of respect and as a way of thanking her for the advice she had offered me over the years.

"Do you remember Robert?"

"Sure, we went snowboarding together last year." Robert and I had met at a Grateful Dead show at Red Rocks in Colorado in 1983. We hit it off and stayed in touch. The next year he arrived in New York to get his MBA at Columbia University. He was an avid smoker and, like me, was a big fan of LSD. If one of us ever ran out we could always count on the other for some clean doses. He came from a wealthy, dysfunctional family and was as radical left as they came. Surprisingly, as soon after he got his master's, he made an uncharacteristic decision to move out to Sacramento to take a job working for Wells Fargo. After that we only saw each other at Dead shows or on ski trips whenever we could get it together to schedule one.

"He will be a part of this too." Her arm flashed in front of my face as she pointed to a place to turn off. We can talk more later, pull over here." We were on an empty stretch of road and I pulled into a turn-around near a bridge that went over a small river. "I just got off the plane and drove straight here, I need to stretch my 1egs."

As we walked, I thought about my lack of surprise when I found that Rose knew Robert. Ever since I met her, she had seemed to exercise her will in all areas of my life. I don't know how they knew each other, and for all I know she may have engineered our meeting. The woman who had brought us together turned out to be an old friend of Rose's. She had offered to give me a ride from the campground to the show, and when I got in her VW van, Robert was there. We were both tripping our faces off, and fairly out of our minds, so we didn't talk much. We kept running into each other throughout the show, but it wasn't until sunrise when we ran into each other in the campground that we actually spoke and introduced ourselves.

Years later, Rose invited me over to her apartment and Robert was sitting on her couch. Her knowing Robert seemed natural, as she had spun her web intricately through the details of my life. No sooner had I arrived when she announced that now would be a good time to get naked, and proceeded to give us a slow striptease. She used her sexiness and her body as a way of breaking down social barriers and building bonds. She always said that she felt more comfortable with a person after she had made love to them. I think it was a form of control for her. She made love to both of us, somehow making us both feel like we had her complete attention.

When we had gotten a half mile from the road, Rose sat down on a large rock that jutted out into the stream at the top of a small waterfall. The pungent, piney aroma of the sugary California air exploded in our brains as the warmth of the sun penetrated our bodies. I lit a joint and asked her why she thought the timing was good to do something big. She had always advised me to stay under the radar of the authorities, who were focused on catching importers and large traffickers. I was curious why she would now recommend otherwise.

"You know the stock market crashed last week? We think that the crash will give us the political clout we need to get the ball rolling on a plan to take the heat off. We have been waiting for a number of people to sign on, and this latest bit of news seems to have done the trick." She paused and looked me in the eye, "It will be risky, but it will be fun."

I had never paid much attention to the stock market and wasn't sure how it might play into Rose's plan, or even what the plan was besides the obvious selling of more weed. I also knew that she liked to maintain a certain amount of mystery, both as womanly allure and as a shrewd protection for all those involved. I understood that illegal operations often work best when information is shared on a strict "need to know" basis and kept in cells, but to find out how much she was willing to reveal I asked her about the "we" she referred to.

"You, Nathan, Robert, myself and some others whom you will probably never meet."

I knew Nathan through Rose. They were the same age and had met when they were both attending NYU in the late '60s. Nathan was tall, dark and handsome, a real lady-killer. Rose had told me that they had an intense fling when they had first met. She said he was a consummate lover and the size of his ego was matched by his sexual endowment. When they were together you could feel the tension caused by a powerful attraction balanced by a strongly enforced distance between these two massive personalities.

Nathan was charming and intelligent. He carried himself in a regal manner that was quite convincing. Shrewd and determined, one could imagine him easily achieving any goal he set his mind to. He spoke eloquently and had a wealth of knowledge to back up his points of view. Where the strength of his character came from was a mystery to me; it was as if he really had all the answers.

Rose took off her shirt, leaned back on the rock and continued, "We are going to buy as much product as we can out here and ship it back to New York. It will be your job to bring the cash back out to Robert. That cash will end up deposited in bank accounts we will set up for the growers. Also, I want you to help develop the distribution network back east. Besides servicing all your own clients, I want you to help me set up a delivery service. I have an idea for a bike messenger service that will deliver ounces to people right in their offices. I think that the wealthy smokers, lawyer and broker types, will be receptive to the Californian buds, and if we are smart, we can greatly increase our sales. I know that you have a lot of younger friends that might be interested in making some money, so I want you to recruit as many messengers as you trust. We will set it up so they make a couple of hundred dollars a day and they won't be working very hard." She paused and threw her head back and shook out her hair. I knew it was a wig, but it was still sexy as hell and it made her tits dance in the sun.

"I was looking at uniforms the other day."

"Uniformed delivery of weed?" I asked, knowing that whatever Rose did she did all the way, and with style.

"Yes, I think we should jack up the price and have employees show up looking crisp."

"Most of the peeps I know that would jump on the gig are long-hairs or dreaded out."

"That is fine; they will look hip as long as the uniform is stylish and they don't smell too badly." She smiled as she said that, probably thinking of the hippies that sold weed in Washington Square Park.

"I will certainly do what I can to help." Actually, at that moment I had more attention on her naked chest than I did on what she was saying. I tried to cover up, "How is Robert going to get away with depositing large amounts of cash?"

"Don't worry, it's all worked out, and you don't want to know."

Of course, I really did want to know, but what she was saying was that she wasn't going to tell me. "How will you convince the growers to sell all their weight to us?"

"You'll see at the meeting," she said, tiring of my questions. She rolled onto her side and, reaching for my crotch, asked, "Feeling the call of the wild?"

"Uh huh."

We stripped off the rest of our clothes and stood admiring each other. In a rush of excitement, our hands became a blur over one another's body. She pulled me into her while we stood on the rock. With one foot on the ground and the other wrapped around my backside, she clung to me, staring into my eyes and rocking back and forth.

Rose doesn't reach a peak quickly; it's a slow, steady ascent that culminates in a flurry of moans and convulsive caresses. She is very vocal and talks some serious trash when she feels so inclined. Playful with her sexuality, she enjoys taking on different persona, sometimes passive and at other times quite dominating. She makes a habit of dressing in a style that alerts her partner to her preference of the day. Over her short, butch haircut she wore wigs, of which she had many styles. With her extensive wardrobe and her wigs, she easily changes her look from schoolgirl to dominatrix and anything in between with ease. She is an extremely exciting woman and a passionate lover, and it is only with the control she has taught me that I could hold off my own release.

On the rock, under the slippery sun, she was letting me be the aggressor, urging me on with little gasps and her most innocent-looking face. She let herself fall into a constant swoon as I supported her weight while she shook in delight. She had climaxed twice and sensed me close when she pulled away.

"Save it for later, big boy," she said, giving my hardness a playful slap. Then she jumped into the cold mountain stream for a rinse and I followed her in, which put a quick end to my excitement. After our refreshing dip we dried ourselves in the warmth of the sun on the rock.

Chapter Two

With faces flush from the passion we had shared, we continued on to the meeting at a restaurant that was apparently partially owned by one of the growers in attendance. I felt totally focused and all my senses were sharp. I was glad I had not released my energy, as my mind was as clear as the mountain stream. Neither of us spoke as we watched the countryside slip by. The hum of the engine was like the "Om" of universal consciousness, and the scented air of the warm day and the tree-covered hills dancing past the windows enchanted our brains.

We arrived at the restaurant and found Nathan with a half dozen other men. I had trimmed for three of them and knew they grew a lot of weed and assumed the others did as well. Rose knew them all. After the greetings and my introduction, we all sat down. I was introduced as "Banjo," which was the name I used when I worked as a trimmer. The restaurant was empty except for us and the growers wondered why they had been summoned.

Nathan started in. "I am pleased you all could make it. Rose and I have a plan that we would like to propose to you and we are confident you will find it interesting. To get right to the point, we want to buy all of your product. In fact, we want you to grow more and bring us all the product you can get from your friends."

Charlie Freedom, a mountain of a man who spoke in soft tones, said, "We are already growing as much as we feel comfortable with and have no problem selling it. If you want the exclusive, you will have to make it worth our while." Freedom, as Charlie was called, finished his sentence looking Rose right in the eyes. He was a bit of a mystic and felt that he could see someone's future when he looked in their eyes. A bystander might have misinterpreted his staring as a challenge, but I knew they went way back and trusted each other implicitly.

Freedom was one of those old acid heads whose mind worked on a different plane from the rest of us. He was a vegan, Buddhist, member of the Rainbow Family, and totally anti-establishment. He had been a radical back in the '60s, but had mellowed with age and now spent most of his time in the mountains with his plants. Rose had introduced me to him on my first trip out and I had trimmed for him for eight weeks. He was happy to share his world view with anyone who would listen and my interest had flattered him. We developed a tight bond over that first eight weeks that continued through the years.

"How much are you selling for now?" Rose asked.

Big Jim, who was a small guy, chimed in, "$2800 a pound down in San Francisco."

"We will pay you $3000, and pick it up at your door," said Rose, "and we will always pay the highest going price."

Freedom asked if we had a plan to transport the weed out of town. "You are talking about a lot of volume. We usually make a lot of small trips and stay out of the headlines by doing so."

"We will take care of that," Nathan said, "but there is more to this plan. I know you guys have a lot of cash lying around and we want to offer you a way to clean it up, with one caveat."

We all knew that Nathan had connections to bankers and other finance people, as he had done a stint as a V.P. at a large international bank back in New York in the early '80s. He was also bred into the financial world that impresses its ideals onto the rest of the world. Born in Litchfield, Connecticut, a bastion of very old, very conservative money, he was raised and educated to become a member of the financial ruling class. His parents, who had made hundreds of millions from the millions they had inherited, had sent him to the finest schools. From St. George's Prep he went on to Yale, where he mingled with his peers in high style. It was rumored that while at Yale he was a member of the Skull and Bones that was known for churning out high-level corporate players and politicians.

After graduating from Yale he moved to New York to attend NYU Law School. It was there that he had been attracted to the radical student organizations and met Rose. Because of his conservative upbringing, when he first attempted to join the SDS he was viewed as a plant or a spy. Only his ability to give moving speeches and his willingness to think big allowed him to earn his status as a member. It was really the gravity of a confused zeitgeist that brought Nathan and the SDS together, and it worked out as more of a co-existence, with most members maintaining their suspicions. But Nathan wasn't satisfied with the modus operandi of the group. The SDS was committed to change, but saw it as a continuous struggle to be engaged by peaceful means. These methods were too slow and cumbersome for Nathan, who wanted to make big statements and hurt the system so their causes would be recognized. His ranting contributed to the formation of a splinter group, the Weather Underground, that went on to build bombs and try to make things happen, by force. It was partially through the acts of the Weather Underground and other members of the militant left that led to the derailment of the momentum that had grown during the '60s. Combined with rampant drug use and an agenda that was much too broad, the movement fell apart after its significant gains in the area of civil rights. Many of the members of the SDS saw his actions as contributing to their eventual dissolution, which confirmed their suspicions of his malicious intent.

"What's the vig?" asked one of the growers.

"No vig," said Rose. "You will get a dollar in the bank for every dollar you put up. The caveat is that you have to invest the money into stocks that we recommend. You might lose money on some of the stocks, but profits from the others should make up for any losses. Even if your portfolio goes down some, it won't be the usual thirty to fifty percent it would normally cost you to bring your money above board."

Justin spoke next. He doesn't speak very often, but people respect his ideas and listen to what he says. He had acquired a law degree and an M.B.A. before leaving his busy life to live off the grid in the mountains. His house was miles into the woods and fully powered by solar and wind power. He ate only food that he grew, going so far as to bring his own produce with him on vacation. He was the only grower who was clean-cut and clean-shaven, and although he lived beyond the reach of civilization, he was quite worldly.

"I don't know what the kid is doing here, but the rest of us have worked together on large projects in the past. You are suggesting that we turn over tens of millions of dollars to you. Even when we were running boatloads of Colombian, it rarely went over a few million dollars. This sounds a little scary."

"First of all, I vouch for Banjo here. His being at this meeting shows that Nathan and I give him our full approval. Secondly, you say you are scared of money in the bank when meanwhile you have so much money buried underground, you probably can't remember where it all is." The growers all laughed with recognition of the accuracy of Rose's statement. "I can't do more than give you my assurance that your money will reach the bank unquestioned, and will be well documented. The investments will be selected for you and all you have to do is write the checks to your broker. Once the money is in the bank in your name it's legit; we just want to be able to direct your investments."

"Seems a little sketchy and more than a little complicated. I have always tried to keep my business as simple as possible," said Freedom. "Keeping it simple keeps it safe."

"And it sounds like we lose control of our money," said

Big Jim.

Nathan assured them, "Yes, you will lose control of your money, but you can pull out at any time, with no hard feelings and a bunch of clean money."

"With all that cash going to the same place, won't it raise some eyebrows?" asked Big Jim.

"It's one of those 'better if you don't know' things. But we have as good a system as one could hope for. The state will look the other way and the feds will only know about the capital gains on your investments. Some of the players have a lot to lose and are very anxious to remain unknown soldiers in this fight."

Nathan saw everything as win or die. I could see how his passion would be convincing to a student group or corporate board, but I wasn't sure what the soldiers were fighting for nor why they would take the risk, beyond the obvious desire to have ever increasing amounts of money.

"Further, there won't be any helicopters looking for your fields next year. I assure you that you can grow ten times as much next season. I know there is a level of secrecy here that makes you feel uncomfortable, but it is for the best. We have been through a lot together in the last twenty years and you guys should have a pretty good idea of how I think. I am very careful and very contrived. I wouldn't get you guys involved if I didn't feel comfortable with it myself. You know I have some connections that I never talk about and a lot of this plan is coming through those channels. You remember the time I drove the impounded boat full of hash right out of the customs impound yard? Well, this deal is going down with that level of connections." Nathan was on a roll. He had the gleam in his eye and his tongue was dancing. If he wanted to convince you that he could move the sun, he would probably succeed.

"We have a high level of trust here, but you are asking a lot," said Freedom.

I was sure that Nathan and Rose were not going to give up any more information and it began to look like it was going to be a very long meeting. Based on the reluctance I felt in the room, I was becoming convinced that the growers wouldn't go for it, when Justin spoke up.

"I'm in." Everyone looked at him with surprise and he continued, "Obviously, there is some grand plan here. We all know that Nathan has one foot in the sub-culture camp and the other in the ruling elite's polo grounds, and this smells of both. And, I would walk over hot coals if Rose suggested it." He added, with a smile to Rose, "I have no more questions. Just tell me what to do."

It took a little more talking through, but the other growers held Justin in such high esteem that they too came around. In the end, they were all on-board.

"We have people counting on this year's crop, so we can't sell it all to you, but we can try to buy as much as we can from our neighbors. And when planting season comes around next year you can give us confirmation about the lack of helicopters, and we will grow more than you can handle."

Nathan spoke up. "I doubt that, because demand is increasing greatly. I think in a couple of years the market for Mex will dry up completely. Demand will decrease because your product is so much better, and the supply will dwindle due to increasing pressure at the border in an attempt to keep the dollars here. There is a lot of concern about the amount of money that is crossing the border, perhaps more than the devastating effect the hard drugs are having. There is also a greater upside to all this. We fully expect that the stocks that will end up in your portfolios to be over-achievers. So you will probably end up making more money from the investments than you ever would have from marijuana alone. I know that paying taxes and having your money documented goes against your grain, but you all should find an accountant that you trust. It's a new way of thinking for you off-the-grid types, but when it's legal money that is what you have to do."

"Well, what's the where, when and how of it?" asked Freedom.

"Where do you think the best place to back up a truck is around here?"

All eyes were on me. I hadn't spoken yet and the growers seemed to be sizing me up. The three I had previously met all liked me, but were surprised to see me in such a place of trust. The others checked Rose and Nathan's faces and received confident affirmation.

Breaking the silence, Rose ventured, "We were all young once, and Banjo here is the next generation. Nathan and I won't be able to come out here that much, so Banjo will pick up the product and bring the money to the bank. He will open the accounts and deliver the paperwork for you to sign. I trust him not to look at the paperwork to see your real names, and you do want to use your real names. Once you mail the forms back to the bank, you can open a brokerage account anywhere you like. We will send word with Banjo about which stocks you should buy."

"You have a lot of trust in our young friend," said Big Jim.

"I have an eye for good people." Rose gave him one of those ribbings that remind people of their past.

"All that is good, but he is talking about a truck. You can't fill a truck in Garberville and expect to make it very far. We would lose even before we start. The local police are pretty relaxed, but the same isn't true for the state troopers."

"We have it all worked out," said Rose, "and..."

"We know, it's better if we don't know," said Justin. "We will work out a spot. Just send word when we should expect young Banjo here. The harvest is all in and the trimmers are working, so give us a few weeks and we will be ready."

I suggested we take some sooner to prime the pump and get advance orders. "I have a friend in L.A. who does a lot of this type of product and I think he can be very helpful. I think I should bring fifty pounds or so back to New York and another fifty to LA. Between the two cities, we should be able to do a few hundred pounds a week to start."

"That is a lot of weed!" exclaimed one of the growers who hadn't spoken yet. "Probably a quarter of the production in the triangle. You're talking about over fifty million dollars!"

"We will do what we can this year," I said, "and next year we will do more. Hopefully, a lot more." I was in over my head, but I was cocky and knew the potential was there and wasn't afraid to try to make it happen. The growers didn't know what to think. If I hadn't been with Rose and Nathan and had spoken such large numbers, they would have written me off as reckless and run me out of town. As it was, I impressed them with my bravado and calm. "Now we know you guys have expenses, and though it will only take a week or two to sell the first load, I will bring a significant down payment back with me. If I take a hundred pounds, that will be $300,000, so I will try to bring a million when I come back." Now it was Rose and Nathan's turn to be surprised, though they hid it well. They had expected me to follow their lead, and here I was pushing the agenda by talking about a truck and cash.

The truth was that I had been thinking about running trips from California to New York for years. It was my fourth year coming out to trim and I knew the kind Californian buds would become a big market if I could bring it to town in serious quantities. Unknown to them, I had already worked out a plan to get hundreds of pounds at a time shipped back east, and had enough cash to buy a load on my own. When Rose had said that the trucking was all worked out, she had simply been following my lead, and when I mentioned money, she knew that I had a few hundred thousand and that she could match it. The growers were willing to front, but we all realized that the sooner we got them some money, the more of this year's harvest we could get.

We left the restaurant satisfied on all sides. The growers asked a few more questions about growing more next year and Nathan sent them off with dollar signs rolling in their eyes. It wasn't just the money that excited the growers; marijuana growers get a lot of satisfaction from the growing itself, just like most farmers. They take a lot of pride in their creations and enjoy nothing better than standing in the middle of a field of plants that receive their love. Nathan's mention of the authorities easing up next year had them all imagining growing larger fields than they had ever considered.

When they had all left, Nathan followed Rose and me over to her car. They stood staring at me.

"I guess you guys want to know about the truck." They nodded. "Well, I didn't expect either of you out here and certainly didn't know about some 'grand plan.' As for myself, I planned to buy up as many pounds as I could this year and bring it back to New York. I guess we are all on the same page."

"Well, what's your plan?" asked Nathan.

"Is my plan *our* plan?"

Nathan looked at Rose and seemed to agree on some last piece of the puzzle. "Yes, you, Rose and I will be equal partners... New York and L.A."

He looked at Rose and me for approval. I figured that whatever we would do would be bigger than what I could do alone, and Rose thought equal partners would make the accounting easier than any other arrangement. Rose and I would deal with the distribution and Nathan would deal with the political stuff, and we would all direct as much business as we could to the retail delivery service idea Rose had going. Partners it was.

"How are you going to get the product out of Northern California?"

"Twice a week a refrigerated truck comes up from San

Francisco to deliver organic juices to the local stores. It is usually empty on its return trip, but it won't be anymore. The driver is someone my dad knew when he was in college, a Vietnam vet and a solid dude. My cousin Carla got him the job as she is the shipping coordinator for a large beverage supply company with a distribution center in an industrial park in South San Francisco. She will pack it up and ship it to wherever we need it to go. She runs the dock and can go in on weekends when she is there by herself, so it should work smoothly. We will pay all the freight charges on a separate account, and so as long as her supervisor doesn't notice some missing shipping supplies, we should be fine. The truck travels Tuesdays and Fridays, so if we fill it Friday the loading dock is all ours for the weekend. On Monday the shipping company will pick it up, and it's on the way to New York."

Nathan said he wanted to talk through the shipping details further, but it could wait. Then he said, "Now I'm off to a dinner engagement in Sonoma County and then driving to Sacramento late tonight. I have a golf date with Robert's boss from the bank and a certain bank auditor from the state finance department. I'll see you two back in the Big Apple."

"Who calls it the Big Apple?" I thought. It has become a common vernacular, but almost nobody knows why. It turns out that jockeys down south referred to prize money at the track as apples and when they caught wind of the winnings in New York they dubbed it The Big Apple.

Rose and I drove back to Little Bear's house through the dripping California sunshine. The air was richly perfumed with the scent of ponderosa and redwood. We spoke no more of the plan that day, just enjoyed the scenery. Dylan's 'Blood on the Tracks' was playing on the Jaguar's awesome sound system. When 'Shelter from the Storm' came on, I lit a joint and inhaled deeply.

Nice car, I thought. I think I need a West Coast car too.

Chapter Three

When we arrived back at Little Bear's mountain home it was mid-afternoon. Rose wasn't planning to stay. She had dinner plans down in Berkeley at Chez Panisse, one of her favorite restaurants in the world. She gave me a hug and a sloppy kiss and started for the driver's-side door. I held her back, suggesting that maybe we had something to finish. She came back teasingly into my embrace and rubbed her pelvis against mine. She apologized, but she really had to go. I told her she was leaving me in a tense situation and pleaded with her to reconsider.

"Maybe one of the cuties who are trimming with you will help you out."

"I haven't had any interest yet, and you know I never chase 'em."

"You might be surprised what a little competition will do. I assure you that my attention did not go unnoticed."

She was right. I ended up spending the night with Karen. She had a law degree, was a major Deadhead, and a veritable sexual gymnast. Karen teased me about Rose, and though she knew I was lying when I told her that I had been saving myself for her, the act of flattery had the desired effect. We ended up spending every spare minute over the next two weeks in each other's arms. When Little Bear's crop was all manicured, she told me to look her up if I was ever in Santa Cruz. Otherwise, she'd see me at New Year's or on spring tour, as she didn't miss many West Coast Dead shows.

I drove down the mountain and met with Big Jim to get the hundred pounds that would help to spark the demand. We met at a coffee shop/bookstore in town and I followed him out to his stash spot. We didn't talk much while we filled my trunk, but when we were done he asked if I wanted to smoke a joint before I hit the road. I don't like to smoke in the car when I am transporting a load, so I gladly accepted his invitation.

"How did you meet Rose?" he asked, handing me the joint he had rolled.

"She approached me at a gallery where Jean Michele Basquiat was having an opening party. Like most people there, I had gone to get laid. When she singled me out, I felt like I had won the door prize."

"A very sexy woman indeed. Please don't take offense, but I am surprised to see someone so young having made their way as far into her confidence as you seem to have done."

"Is twenty-one so young? I have been old enough to go to war for three years now; thank god Reagan hasn't gotten us into one yet," I said defensively as he handed me the joint.

"Jesus, twenty-one. You are younger than I thought."

I didn't say anything anymore. I realized how stupid I sounded with my remark. I knew it was useless, even self-defeating, to try to convince an older person of one's maturity. The best sign of wisdom is often silence, so I sat quietly smoking, waiting to see what Jim would say next.

I have always looked older than I am. By sixteen years old I already showed thick facial hair, and have looked to be in my mid-twenties ever since. It worked to my advantage mostly, but occasionally I found myself in situations that I wasn't emotionally prepared for. Selling weed was certainly not one. I looked Jim confidently in the eyes.

"Rose told me you have a very old soul," he said, returning my stare as I handed him the joint.

He continued, "She is an excellent judge of character, so I imagine she has her reasons for bringing you so far into this. I've seen her in action; she picked me out of the crowd fifteen years ago." Drawing thick smoke from the perfectly rolled joint into his lungs he got a smile and said, "Let me guess, she already seemed to know all about you and what makes you tick before even speaking to you."

"It was kind of weird," I said. Jim was in his mid-thirties and had a very peaceful spirit. Rose had told me that when she met him, he was very inspired, but without direction. She turned him on to acid and Picasso and Dali and sparked his talents. Supported by his green thumb, he had become an accomplished painter whose work was well received in the galleries of San Francisco. "I was seventeen when we first met, and within a few weeks we had done a few truckloads. I don't know what made her trust me. Thinking back I wonder if I was worthy or if I became so under her trusting guidance."

Jim finished my thought. "She sees potential and isn't afraid of becoming involved. Definitely not shy of intimacy, she takes time and responsibility. She uses her ability to read people to help others become actualized. I think she cares very deeply about humanity. Sometimes I wonder if the marijuana business holds her back from doing more, and other times I think it is an excellent vehicle for her."

"She does seem to help a lot of people," I said. "I know I've learned a lot from her. Did she give you a reading list, too?"

"A reading list, meditation instruction, taught me about my sexuality and many other things."

"You guys were lovers?"

"Yes, and I wouldn't be half the lover I am without the training she put me through."

"Training is a good word for it. I am just finishing my training. She wants me to spend more time with lovers my own age."

"Don't be surprised if she wants to join in."

Somehow knowing that we had both been so strongly influenced by Rose made us feel closer than one would expect after having only met twice.

We finished the joint and the buzz was washing over us in waves of sensory candy. We sat on his balcony, basking in the refulgence of the autumnal noon sun. The valley below flowed away from us to a distant canyon to the east, a verdant landslide of technicolor. The tops of the pines danced in the wind in a coniferous ballet that tattooed the air with sublime serenity. Painting myself into the scene, my mind soared with volant spirit until the sound of Jim's voice brought me back.

"I guess you should probably get going."

I could have sat there for days, but he was right. I had a redeye to catch back to the East Coast, and had to meet my friend Simon from L.A. to hand off some of the pounds to him. We were meeting at a mutual friend's house up on Grizzly Peaks in Berkeley around six o'clock. We had spoken briefly about the meeting, and I was anxious to let him know about the quantities I would soon be able to supply. It was a long drive south, so I took my leave from Jim and turned my rental car toward the highway.

I had rented a four-door sedan that I hoped would blend into the traffic unnoticed. I was thankful that the car had a cassette player and I put in a live recording of the Dead at Madison Square Garden in '83 and locked the cruise control to fifty-five. Karen had given me the tape when I realized the car had a tape player, and listening to Jerry's glistening licks I thought of her. She was a sweet girl and quite comfortable with her sexuality. I found that many of the women my age were so confused about sex they could hardly even enjoy themselves, much less rock my world. I looked forward to spending time with her on my trips out west. As the road slipped under my wheels, I wondered how Rose had known that her attention would spark the interest of the women I was trimming with. I guess it made me more attractive, or increased my social value, or it was a smell thing. All I know is that I love women in all their unpredictability and have no hope of ever figuring them out.

Thinking about the business at hand, I started making plans for when I got back to New York. I wanted to move the first fifty pounds as quickly as possible so I could return in a few days for a big load. I knew the growers would be busy selling through their usual channels and the longer I took, the less weed would be available. I had a couple of people lined up, but I would have to hustle the rest.

The juice truck made the trip on Tuesdays and Fridays, and I was aiming for Tuesday of next week. I knew it was easier for my cousin if it was on the weekend, but I wanted to get started and figured we could work at night. It was Thursday so I knew that I only had the weekend, hoping to catch a flight back on Sunday. Many of the dealers I worked with attempted to have "normal" lives and only operated during the week, so I had to max out my schedule on Friday. I could also spread some samples under the guise of weekend social calls to those who were at home with their families.

When I got to Berkeley, I grabbed a hippie burrito at a spot just off Telegraph, where I could keep an eye on the car. The hill was buzzing with its usual detritus of subculture fallout. Healthy, fairly sane hippies and punks in need of a bath led a comfortable vagabond life in the benevolent climate. I thought of the homeless people in New York City, most of them half-crazy and the rest drunk on cheap wine, bearing the brunt of the Northeast's harsh winters. Berkeley was a much better place to be homeless. It was an attractive lifestyle choice for most of these kids who were in their teens and tweens.

As I headed out to my car, I noticed a skinny white kid wearing tie-dye and sporting ass-length dreadlocks, waking up from a midday nap. He and his two dogs appeared to be living in a late-model Volvo station wagon with Massachusetts plates. I pictured his parents in a large colonial house in a respectable neighborhood writing checks they thought were going to tuition and rent. As I walked by, he asked me if I wanted to buy some 'shrooms. I bought an ounce for my friend on Grizzly Peaks as a gift, and headed up the hill.

Simon was already there when I pulled in. Having not seen each other in almost a year, we gave each other a big hug, and shared our excitement that we would have more hang time because of the biz. He knew he would make a killing on the fifty pounds I brought him, and when I told him there was a lot more to come, he got ecstatic.

"How are you managing to get your hands on so much of Cali's finest?"

"Simple, I told them that I will always be the highest bidder. I don't think these guys realize the goldmine they are sitting on, I bet the wholesale price goes up fifty percent in the next few years. And you know what? We will still make money. Retail price is what? $250 an ounce now? I bet once people find out how good these buds are, they will pay double that."

Simon added, "Don't you go pushing the price up. I like the numbers where they are. When will I see you?"

"In the next week, week-and-a-half. Listen, try and get all the cash you can together for my next trip. While I have the growers' attention, I want to get as much of this year's crop as possible. One of the things they like about the deal I have with them is they won't have to transport their product anymore, and when I pull into town with a truck next week, I want to fill it as much as possible. So you know, empty the safe-deposit box, borrow, presell...whatever you can."

"You got it. And now, I am out of here."

"No fatty for the ride?"

Simon, being more cautious than I, didn't even like to drive stoned when he was transporting, so he declined and drove off. He had a long ride ahead of him and probably wouldn't reach his place in Santa Monica until around midnight.

I had to return the rental car, so I smoked a joint and headed to the airport. Once my luggage was checked, I commenced drinking in hopes of sleeping through the transcontinental flight.

I love flying. That existential feeling you get sitting in an airport as the out-of-focus public address system blathers on about departure times to destination after destination. The potential energy is intense. Down this gangway go to Cleveland, the next to Alaska, another might go to another continent. I have never tried it, but I wondered if I would get the same feeling even if I wasn't bound to walk down one of the jet ways. The potential is there, so much potential.

I also felt as if the airlines were there to service my illegal business. It was the safest way to travel while transporting weed. The cops never looked at national flights, and the airlines were happy to have the business and never looked twice at you. I usually flew business class. I always used a different assumed name, bought my tickets with cash, and since you never needed to show identification, I felt totally incognito. I filled my luggage with weed and checked it with the airline and never even had an increase of pulse rate.

Chapter Four

I sat back in my heavily cushioned seat in business class and was prepared to pass out when I heard someone with a thick New York accent and a gravelly voice call my name. I was a little concerned because it wasn't the name I had bought a ticket under, but luckily the attendant didn't hear. It was Tom, the closest to a gangster I had ever met in the weed business. He asked my neighbor to switch seats with him in a way that couldn't be refused and sat down next to me.

Tom was six feet two inches with broad shoulders, and a bit of a paunch. He looked like a cop. He spoke like a cop. That is because he had been on the New York City narcotics squad for ten years before he pocketed $150,000 from a drug bust and got caught. It hadn't been the first time, but it was his last. The feds had set him up, and he went down. He did eight years, which eroded what was left of the line between cop and criminal. Most of the people in the biz were good people, gentle and generous, and felt they were doing a service for their friends. Tom was closer to a thug, or a cocaine dealer, and his years of carrying a gun set him apart from the hippies who populated the industry.

When he got out of jail, he put the cash that he had stashed together with the connections he made in jail and started running trips of Mexican weed up from Arizona. He had partnered up with a guy who had been Rose's boyfriend when I first met her, and I had met Tom a few times. Luckily, Rose kept her dealings in a discreet manner, so he had no idea to what extent I was involved. I had run into him a few times around town and he always offered to supply me, but I always declined. I tried to play it like I was just doing small deals, but he didn't go for it. It was actually a little comical how it worked out. He kept making his offer sweeter and sweeter, thinking it was his prices that turned me off. He misinterpreted my reluctance to work with him and assumed that I was into much bigger action than I was. His last comment of our conversation had been, "Damn you're big." I tried to convince him otherwise, but he wasn't having it. I guess due to his confusion, he was always trying to impress me. Before the plane even took off, he was talking loudly. I knew there was no way I was going to get any sleep, so I joined him in keeping the attendant busy as a cocktail waitress. This guy was insane. He was talking about his smuggling operation with little attempt to keep the conversation private. Even when he attempted to whisper, it only served to catch more attention and his ranting was heard throughout the cabin. I had never been more thankful that I used a fake name.

When we were somewhere over Kansas, he switched his topic of conversation from smuggling to attempted murder. He was actually bragging about getting somebody shot at, confirming my initial instinct not to work with him. In his nasally, cop-voice he asked, "Do you remember Eugene from the Upper East Side?" I nodded. "Well, that conniving little prick tried to steal some of my customers, so you know what? I had him shot."

I tried to sound tough. "You had him offed?"

"No, but I tried. That lucky bastard actually survived! Check this out. I went uptown and hired two Westies who would shoot anybody for a couple of grand, and told them to unload a clip each into that thieving fuckhead. I drove them down to Eugene's block and parked across the street. They stood outside his building until one of Eugene's customers came out. I recognized the kid as one of my old customers who didn't work with me anymore, and gave the Westies a flick of my headlights. They grabbed the poor hippie kid, who I am sure wet his pants, and told him to ring the bell and say he forgot something. They got in the building, and I stuck around to make sure they finished the job.

"A few minutes later I am sitting in my car watching the door and I see the Westies come out and give me a nod to let me know they had done the job. I don't know why, but I stuck around to see what would happen next. All of a sudden, the kid comes out screaming for help. I was about to drive off when Eugene comes crashing out the door and falls on the sidewalk. He gets up and whips off his jacket and you know what? You'd never guess. The bastard is wearing a vest. That fucker took eighteen shots to the chest and didn't lose a drop of blood. I think he was going to chase the guys until the pain set in. It doesn't kill you, but getting shot wearing a vest still hurts like hell. The hippie kid ran off and when people started to gather around Eugene, he grabbed his jacket and went back inside."

He had clearly enjoyed the moment. He seemed more impressed with Eugene's survival than the failure of his plan. Slapping his leg he said, "Amazing. Eighteen shots and no blood."

I asked if he would try again.

"No. I think he got the message. I paid the Westies the rest of their money anyway. They couldn't believe it either. Eighteen shots. Damn, it was his lucky day."

I had always imagined that all pot dealers were peaceful cats. Pot is so relaxing. The problem was, Tom didn't smoke. I was happier than ever that he didn't know my business.

We got to New York and he gave me his phone number and told me to call him when the Mex started rolling. I told him I wasn't working much, just trying to finish college. He didn't believe me and said, "Just call me."

I grabbed my suitcases and poured myself into the back of a cab. I awoke to the cabbie banging on the window to wake me up in front of my house in the West Village. I got upstairs and barely got undressed before passing out.

The weekend was a blur. Between lack of sleep, a busy schedule, and constant smoking of kind bud, the days blended into a kaleidoscope of events. I cashed out thirty pounds and gave twenty to Rose. We were both surprised and excited by the increased enthusiasm for the Cali weed and knew we could corner this apparently growing demand.

On Sunday I met with Nathan and Rose to discuss our operation. We brunched at the Odeon, a swanky bistro in Lower Manhattan. The Odeon was one of the first establishments to brave the dead-zone of Tribeca. Its art-deco decor and Parisian feel attracted businessmen and politicians by day and artists and the club crowd at night. Rose loved Paris and by association loved the Odeon. She said it was one of the few places that she felt comfortable eating alone at the bar or taking up a table by herself all afternoon, reading or writing. My schedule was so confused that I skipped the brunch menu and went right for steak-frites and red wine while the other diners had omelets and mimosas.

Afterwards we walked around the corner to the warehouse space Nathan had rented.

Only the three of us and my cousin would know where it was located.

"This neighborhood is perfect," said Nathan. "It is close enough that you can get to it any time and this street is pretty safe. Most of the artist lofts have gone high-end residential, but there is enough commercial traffic that we won't stand out. I will get the supplies we need to make it work. I never thought I would own a pallet jack!"

We christened the space with the sobriquet of 'The Receiving Department'. Nathan would get a pallet jack and all the other necessary tools to make it work smoothly by the time the first load arrived.

"Tell me again about the shipping plan." Nathan asked me.

I was pretty sure he had already checked it all out, but I told him again. He seemed satisfied, but did add that he would supply a little insurance policy to protect the juice truck on its return to San Francisco.

"I think the delivery service is ready to go, we just need some riders," said Rose. She had already rented a storefront and had bought a number of bikes. Her concept was to supply the riders in the morning with a quantity of ounces that were sealed in small retail packages. "Each messenger will be responsible for clearing his account at the end of every day. Money for the sold ounces would be paid and unsold product will be returned. Prices will be set by us, and we will kickstart the client list, but we should also encourage the riders to develop their own clientele. They will get paid on a commission basis and stand to make some good money."

I knew a few friends that were looking for work and would dig the flexibility of this kind of job, and told Rose that I would send them by. She said I should call her with names before I send them by the storefront. The storefront would never have more than a couple of pounds at a time, and would mostly be used to receive phone calls and to page the riders with their destinations. All of us would refer smaller clients to the service.

I left them and went to meet a few clients and canvas the friends who I thought would work well for the delivery service. I found a half dozen eager recruits and told them to go to the storefront Monday morning. I spent the rest of the day in a daze of half sleep, with the constant smoke of either joints or cigarettes filling my lungs. I was planning to jump a plane in the morning and spend a few days with Karen before I headed up north to pick up the load. Part of my reasoning was that it would be better to wait for the truck on Friday so my cousin and I would have the loading dock to ourselves on this first trip. The other reason my plan changed was related to the jones I was feeling for Karen after having spent so much time naked with her over the last few weeks.

When evening rolled around, I went to meet Rose and pick up whatever money she had for the trip. When I got there, she had just finished counting $450,000. With the money I had, I would be able to take over $800,000 with me. That would pay for the hundred pounds we already sold and make a significant down payment on the first load.

"How much will your friend in L.A. have together?" asked Rose.

"Hmm. At least the $160k he owes us and maybe that much again."

"I think it would be a good idea for you to go to L.A. and get his money before you head north. We need as much cash as possible to convince the growers to give us all they can. They can have all the cash this time, but the next trip out there you will see Robert and open the accounts. You also have to make some arrangements for a warehouse in L.A. so we can ship him some of the next load."

"I was going to see a friend for a few days this week."

Rose caught my meaning and teased me. "So you have a 'friend' out west now?"

I told her about Karen and that she had been right about her attention perking interest. She wanted to hear all the details.

"I think you might want to stay focused on business this trip, but maybe she can meet you in L.A. You will probably have some downtime while you are there. If she is all that you say, I want to meet her; I'm sure you wouldn't mind sharing."

Just the thought of sharing Karen with Rose made me hard. I tried to focus on business, as I knew Rose had to split soon and there would be no time for us to be intimate.

"If you fly to L.A. you can pick up the money and rent a space, and make it to Garberville by Thursday. Actually, it is probably better if your new friend doesn't know what you are doing in L.A., so maybe you can put off seeing her until the load is on its way east."

She was right, and I knew I could easily kill a few days in Tinseltown. Karen would have to wait.

"Well, then that's the plan," I said. "I am going to stay at the Beverly Hilton on Monday and Tuesday night at least. If you need to talk to me, I will be under the name Chris Wood."

"Living a little rich, huh?" asked Rose. "The Beverly Hilton?"

"Might as well live rich."

"And why not? I'll get word to Freedom and tell him to expect you on Thursday evening. Have a nice trip. I'll see you when you get back. Oh, and call and tell me when to expect the delivery at The Receiving Department."

I left Rose with sex on my brain. She was dressed provocatively for whatever plans she had that evening, and she looked hot. If I hadn't been so tired, I might have made a move, but in the condition I was in, I could only think about sleep. I headed for home already hearing my pillow calling me.

One problem with driving yourself so hard is that when you finally take time to sleep, it won't come. My exhaustion had seeped into a wired state that kept my mind spinning. I smoked a joint, but that only made me think more, and I lay in bed staring at the ceiling as if I had been doing cocaine all night. Counting on nature's sedative for men, I masturbated, hoping an orgasm would push me over the edge of sleeplessness. To feed my drive, I reminisced about the first time Rose had seduced me.

She invited me to get a massage with her. I had gotten a lot of massages already, but she thought that I should try the Japanese form, Shiatsu. She made an appointment for us at some place in the East 50s, and we headed uptown in a cab. When we arrived, we were shown to separate dressing rooms and stripped down by attentive hostesses. I was a little bashful, but was soothed by the methodical motions of the elderly woman who didn't speak but simply assisted me in stripping down to nothing. Then she offered me a robe and escorted me down the hall to a room where Rose was waiting. The room had a couple of showers along one wall, a hot-tub and a cold-tub, a steam room and a dry sauna. As I was shown in, I saw Rose standing naked under the spray of the shower and as I stepped into the room, my hostess deftly stripped me of my robe and closed the door as she left. Rose laughed at my surprise and told me to relax.

"Being naked is the most natural thing in the world," she said.

I was comfortable being naked, but I was totally intimidated by Rose, and my rising erection caused by the sight of her body added to my apprehension. She turned her body toward me and asked if I wanted to use the steam or the dry sauna first as she massaged her breasts. I stammered something about whatever she thought and asked her if this was part of the massage.

"The older cultures understand what it takes to have a fully relaxing experience, and this is the beginning."

She headed for the dry sauna and motioned me to follow. I tried to be casual, but at eighteen I wasn't so experienced that I felt comfortable with a forty-year-old vixen standing naked in front of me. I had no idea what to expect next. We sat in the sauna and I couldn't hide my excitement. Her body was incredible. I tried not to stare, but she seemed to invite my eyes with the caresses she was giving herself. Finally she asked if I found her attractive. I responded that I imagined anybody would.

"I'm not asking anybody. Do you find me sexy?"

"Absolutely," I responded.

She had a way of asking that made me think she was insecure and hoping to have me confirm her beauty. It made me feel valiant in some way. Her questioning moved me out of my discomfort and dragged me a little out of my shell. We sweated in the dry air as our bodies began to glisten.

"Prove to me that you find me sexy," she said.

"What do you have in mind?"

"I want you to masturbate for me," she urged.

I was totally embarrassed, but somehow, she made me relax and I was soon stroking myself in front of her. She touched herself and spoke seductively as she drew me to the edge. Her casualness with sexuality was maddening and the tone of her voice and her breathy monologue pushed me over the brink into a well of sensation that consumed me from head to toe. She clapped her hands and joyfully congratulated me on overcoming my timid reluctance.

"Let's have a quick rinse and then go to the steam room," she said.

In the fog of the steam bath I found my eyes tracing the outline of her silhouette. I already felt relaxed. She told me that she wanted me to release my energy so I could pay attention to her without losing control. Then she led me out to the hot tub and seduced me in a slow, lustful way. We spent over an hour in the suite before we were called to receive our massages, and when we were done, I felt more relaxed than ever before. I felt completely free of tension and stress.

She introduced me to sex on a new level. The restraint she showed me how to achieve and the sensitivity to my partner's desires she encouraged were the cornerstones of the training she would put me through over the next few years. She was a patient teacher and enforced complete awareness as we made love. If I left the moment and drifted into fantasy, she would gently bring me back, and coached me into being completely present during sex.

I slept like a baby after I finished my recounting of that night. Just before passing out I thought of something Rose had once told me. She said that the sexual act leaving men tired and women revived was crucial to our survival as a species. If it was vice versa, babies would have been left unattended as men constantly mounted sleeping women. I wondered if anthropologists had ever stumbled on that theory.

Chapter Five

I awoke in the morning feeling refreshed for the first time in days. Packing a change of clothes around the bundles of cash in my suitcase, I headed out to the airport. In the late morning I can make it from my corner to Newark airport in less than twelve minutes. Cabs are always easy to catch and fifteen minutes after walking out of my door I was looking at the departures listings for a flight to L.A. American had a non-stop leaving in a little more than an hour, so I went to the check-in desk and bought a ticket for cash under a name I had made up in the cab. I handed over my suitcase and watched $800,000 encased in Samsonite travel down the conveyor belt and disappear into the black hole of the luggage handling department. Rose had given me a copy of Hermann Hesse's "Siddhartha" to read on the flight, and I went to the gate and began devouring the allegorical telling of the life of Buddha.

We were somewhere over the center of the country when I finished the book. Looking out the window I could see the patchwork of farmland that stretched to the horizon under crystal skies. During the fifteen minutes I looked out the window I noticed three different nuclear power plants, with their obvious design coating the landscape with acres of concrete.

There was an elderly gentleman in a business suit sitting next to me who, apparently bored with the figures he had been contemplating, closed his briefcase and engaged me in conversation by asking about the book I had just finished. I gave him a brief synopsis and when he seemed generally interested, I surprised him by making it a gift to him. The act of generosity compelled him to further involve me in conversation. After a few pleasantries we got to the obligatory exchange of titles and job descriptions, as if the information contained in a business card was a window into the essence of a person. I have always seen this as a trivial exchange outside of a business setting, and usually use it as an opportunity to be creative. Of course, being a drug dealer during the height of Reagan's war on drugs, I rarely found it a good idea to announce my current vocation. So I made stuff up. I would try to guess an occupation that would lead my conversational partner to further reveal their character. This trip I decided to be a photographer that did work for Playboy and Penthouse.

"Can you make a good living as a photographer?"

"Yeah, and I get to travel a lot."

"Must make it tough to have a home life. I travel a few times a year and find that it throws off my sense of stability. I don't know how people who travel a lot manage."

"I am a pro at living out of a suitcase; home is wherever my luggage is."

I was surprised. We spoke for the next two hours and he never asked about sex or the women I supposedly took pictures of. He was completely unimpressed and was more curious about my lifestyle and the art of photography than he was about the naked women part. I began to think he might be gay, so I used my secret weapon. I have always found that admitting I am from the West Village, which is a predominantly gay neighborhood, would cause a very noticeable response by someone who was gay or bisexual. He was unfazed. He didn't smoke or drink and seemed to be the most normal, well-adjusted person I had ever met. I was almost jealous of his ability to enjoy a simple, wholesome life.

When the plane touched down at LAX, we said goodbye and wished each other well. I grabbed my suitcase and headed for the rental car counters. Budget had a poster announcing they had a fleet of new Volvo 940's for rent. I thought a car with a little class would be appropriate for my stay in Beverly Hills, so I rented one and hit the freeway.

Driving on "The 5" can be a little hectic with its six lanes of traffic each way and bumper-to-bumper seventy-miles-per-hour insanity, and I had trouble getting in the groove until I was half-finished with my first joint of the day. With a good buzz and the stereo blasting I slipped right into the L.A. driving mode.

Simon lived in Santa Monica a couple of blocks from the beach, so I thought I would stop by and see him before I checked into my hotel. I used the phone at a cafe on Wilshire Boulevard and told him where he could find me. He arrived a half hour later with the finest representation of California beauty one could hope to see. Tanned, with long legs and hair, her presence increased Simon's stature and passersby stumbled into poles and parking meters, unable to take their eyes off her. I stood up and greeted them and Simon introduced me to Sebrina. She seemed sweet and was clearly smitten by Simon. We chatted about literature and politics and drank fruit shakes as we watched the street traffic.

After about an hour Simon suggested to Sebrina that she go and buy an outfit for a party the next night, and she took a wad of cash from Simon and split.

"Well, how did you do?" I asked.

"I was only able to get together a half a mil," he said with a smile. "A couple of people are pretty excited and weren't afraid to put their money up. If you can keep a good supply going, we are going to make a truckload of money."

He knew I was impressed, and we made arrangements for the next day so I could grab the cash. When Sebrina came back, I got up to go as she jokingly asked if she was chasing me off. I assured her that was not the case, but I had other plans.

"Are you coming to the party tomorrow?" she asked.

I looked at Simon, who answered for me that I was. Awesome, I thought. Only in town for a few days and able to catch a party. Simon was down with the "in" crowd, and I knew the party would be a good one, especially during the week. It would only be the real freaks or industry people in-between jobs. I asked how I should dress and realized that I would have to buy something for the affair. I don't like to shop and usually depend on girlfriends to shop with or for me if I can. I said goodbye and headed away from the ocean, with the hills close on my left, through Hollywood to the Beverly Hilton.

I left the suitcase in the trunk, carrying just my carry-on bag, and checked in. The room was comfortable, though the difference between a $50 room and a $450 room is not as great as one might think. A hotel room is a hotel room. Very few establishments have the courage to actually make a statement of style, leaving the rest with the bland feeling of a hotel room. I picked up the phone and asked to be connected to the health spa and was lucky to be able to get an appointment for a massage at four o'clock. This left me time to steam and sauna before my appointment.

When I entered the spa, I was surprised to see Rene. She had been a waitress at The Front, a restaurant around the corner from my house where I would often entertain my friends. We had become good friends during the late-night closings caused by my group's insatiable appetite for food and drink. After the other patrons had left, the staff would often join us and party until dawn. During the two years she had worked there, Rene was attending the Swedish Massage Institute and had moved to L.A. after she graduated. Now, apparently, she worked at the spa at the Beverly Hilton.

I congratulated her on her good fortune, for I was sure she made decent money there.

"Thank you. This is certainly the pinnacle of the trade. I lucked out landing this job just a few weeks after I moved out here. I like my life here, but I miss my friends from back east, and these California people are a little wacky. I still haven't plugged into a social scene. It seems if you don't work in movies, people aren't interested. People say New Yorkers are tough, but I made friends much easier there than I have been able to here. All the driving definitely sucks too. I try and ride my bike to work most of the time, but it is not the same as a pedestrian city."

I felt comfortable with Rene. She knew I sold weed, but was cool enough to never talk about it. Occasionally she would make reference to my lifestyle, but she didn't pass judgment. I asked her if she would have dinner with me that night and she cheerfully accepted.

"Where shall we go?"

"You choose," I told her.

"I get off at seven. I'll meet you in the lobby at seven-thirty and we will take it from there."

After my massage, I walked over to Saks Fifth Avenue, a store I would normally avoid, and bought some clothes. I would rather have patronized some unknown designer, but I didn't have time. Within fifteen minutes I had found two suits that I thought were funky chic that I could wear with a t-shirt and play them down. I also bought a new pair of white tennis sneakers to complete my outfit. It was an abomination to anyone with any fashion sense, I am sure, but to my eyes it made a perfect look for the California scene.

At seven-thirty sharp, Rene put her arm through mine and we headed toward the valet.

"Where to?" I asked.

"Malibu. One of the girls told me about a place called Jeremy's that has good food and overlooks the ocean. Tonight is a full moon; it should be beautiful. It might be expensive, but since you are staying at the Beverly Hilton I figure you can afford it."

"You mind driving?"

"Definitely not," she replied as the valet pulled up in the red Volvo.

The restaurant was excellent. On top of a bluff, a hundred feet above the crashing waves, it had tables outside on a deck from which one could see the moonlight reflected on the frothy waves extending to the horizon. We found ourselves on a second bottle of wine when the meal was over, and were deep in a philosophical conversation.

She had read Steiner, Jung, Campbell, Lacan and many other theoreticians of the modern paradigm and had her own thoughts well ordered. I shot from the hip and trusted my instincts, which proved to be insightful. She had spent a lot more time thinking about such things, but keeping my thoughts focused on compassion and universal empathy I was able to hang. We talked through the second bottle and left the restaurant at closing.

When we got in the car, she asked me if I wanted to eat some mushrooms. She didn't have to work tomorrow and had been wanting to dose since she got out west, but hadn't found a tripping buddy. Always game for a trip, I agreed and we both ate a few caps. I usually prefer to make tea, as it is easier on the stomach, but without the resources we just ate them. She drove us up Topanga Canyon and parked near a tennis court in a cul-de-sac of elegant homes. Her landlady had showed her the spot and they had walked there on a few occasions. We grabbed the jug of water I had in the car and she directed us around the tennis court to a trail that led across the top of a steep caldera. We walked for about a half hour, as the mushrooms kicked in, until we came to the knob of a hill that overlooked all of L.A. to the south and the Valley to the north.

We sat quietly for what must have been an hour or two because I had smoked two joints by myself, as Rene rarely smokes. Taking in the view, it seemed even the stationary lights had trails, as if the spin and orbit of the Earth and the swirling of the Milky Way and the expansion of the universe were all affecting the lights. At one point she asked if she could have a hit of weed so I rolled another joint. When I passed it to her, I noticed her face was a little contorted, like she was about to say something she was sure I wouldn't understand. The weed cracked her open and she vortexed into a cosmological dissertation.

"It all comes down to the inner mind and the outer mind," she said. "The inner mind is connected to our spirit and allows us insight into the workings of the subtle energies. The unknowable. The outer mind reacts to stimuli and dictates the messages to the physical body. We are committed to the physical realm via the workings of our outer mind. Our need to quantify, explain, and understand the world creates such anxiety that we refuse to admit the existence of anything that can't be contemplated by our rational outer mind. This need blocks out all of the instinctive knowledge or transmissions from outside the physical realm. In this transaction we have lost the ability to accept that which is not knowable – our own cosmic nature, or God. The only vestige of this deeper truth left is in the areas where our outer mind has developed fears. Our need to control our environment and make ourselves feel safe keeps an open conduit to our inner mind for information that is relative to our fears. Not just ordinary day-to-day fears, but the ones we grasped in our earliest stages of development that conditioned the way we deal with the world. If that is the only connection we have to our deepest intellect, then perhaps that is the best place to begin our work of reconnecting. Grasping for truth usually makes it unattainable if we force it, but if we simply recognize the channel where it is still functioning, perhaps we can encourage it to grow. Letting go of greed and fear are only the banal, cursory steps on the way to being genuinely helpful in the universe. We must stay tuned to the needs of society, the planet, and the people and conduct our affairs and discourse accordingly. To revel in the bliss of meditation or submerge ourselves in the opiate of luxury is not helpful. We all must find our voice or medium and contribute to the right thinking and right action in all phenomena.

“It is really a question of finding a context with which we can understand the world. The challenge of our modern spiritual selves is to define our relationship to the great unknowable. The old forms are just that, old. We can't trouble ourselves with a redefinition of archaic symbols and myths because the framework that supported those myths has so completely changed. The oldest myths were of gods, from that we moved to a period when humans and gods interacted. As we fell further from our celestial moorings, myths developed about the relation between humans and the physical world. It is no surprise that the modern myths discuss relations between humans and extraterrestrials, as we have exhausted our ability to believe in any divine or animistic phenomena. The challenge now is to create myths, and heroes, that tie us into the deep pockets of our subconscious mind. In order to grow beyond our infantile fears and concerns we need ceremony and clear societal thresholds to move us through the phases of life in a healthy way.

“The constraints we have in our ability to mature are based on perceptions we develop early in life and are never exposed unless actively pursued. The Godhead, Supreme divinity, whatever you want to call it, is within us all. We all have the capacity to adventure to the netherworld and return with the Golden Fleece or elixir that can release us all from our limitations and reveal a fully developed, healthy human persona. Psychology looks to fill the helper role in our individual adventures and guide us or supply the tools that will allow us to slay our own mythical dragons. The church hopes to hand us a complete set of symbols that will usher us from cradle to the grave, even if it is antiquated. If we maintain faith, that symbol set can be effective, but the distance between our perceptions of the world around us, bolstered by scientific thinking that pervades all of society, makes it difficult for its relevance to not come into question.

"Where will the new belief structure come from? Do the old forms have to become so antiquated that they are annihilated before a new context can spring up? The ability to recognize our personal connection to everything, with a capital E, is within us all. To find that truth we need a powerful mode of understanding that will allow us to shed our fears. It all comes down to fear. We develop perceptions of family, community, and the world based on antagonistic and competitive views. This forces us further into our shells and covers our ability to understand a greater relationship. Sometimes I wonder if we must all go through a full cycle of disillusionment and disenfranchisement from ourselves so that we can find our way back, building a more complete self as we go.

"Birth and death; creation, destruction; this Zoroastrian view is so compelling that sometimes I think we might have to perpetually swing between extremes. Isn't there something we can do?"

Somewhere in her litany, I felt myself melting into the rhythmic actions of her voice. The trip was reaching its peak and the visuals were intense. I could see the aural vibration of the scrubby plants that shared our vista and even the ground had its own, visible resonance. The cherry of Rene's cigarette was a red ribbon that streamed through the air as she gesticulated while speaking. Looking at the sky I saw a vast, stippled fabric with perforations that allowed intense beams of light through. When she finally realized I was no longer paying attention, she stopped talking.

After a few minutes of silence she let out a deep breath and said, "Holy shit. I have been so busy talking, I hadn't realized how high I am. I don't think I want to get in the car for a while."

"Last thing on my mind," I said.

As the air grew cooler, we moved closer together. After a while we found ourselves cuddling. It wasn't a prelude to sex;

it was more of an animal instinct that made us act without our being conscious of it. We reclined on each other as puppies or bear cubs might, to shelter us from the damp, chilly air that pushed over the hills from the sea. Our conversation for the next few hours was limited to a few syllables at a time and a lot of giggling. When the sky began to brighten, we were wide-eyed and red-faced, with expressions that made us laugh at each other.

She lived in a guest, or mother-in-law, house she rented from a widow near the top of Topanga, and being too burnt to walk into the Hilton, I crashed at her house for a few hours. I awoke at eleven and found her on the terrace drinking coffee with her cat, Spunky, curled up in her lap. My head was heavy, but I felt thoroughly refreshed. We sat for a while on the terrace in the cool of the morning that already carried the threat of the afternoon heat. I told her I had a party to go to that night and asked her if she would be my date. She accepted, exclaiming that she was not surprised that I would blow into town, where she had been living for a year, with better social contacts than she had.

After going to the Hilton for what turned out to be a $450 shower, I headed toward the beach to meet with Simon.

"You look rough."

"It's part of my style. I'll have you know that even though I look rough, as you are so nice to point out, I feel great. I ended up watching the sunrise in a psychedelic blaze on the top of Topanga. It was awesome. Is it cool if I bring a date to the party tonight?"

"Sure. Anybody I know?"

"You might recognize her; she was a waitress at The Front for a couple of years. She lives out here now. Her name is Rene."

We spent the next few hours counting and straightening out piles of cash, pausing only to roll another joint every now and then.

Chapter Six

From the cars lined up for valet parking we could tell this was going to be a good party. There was hardly a sedan in the group. Racy little Italian sports cars, British coupes, and German speedsters, mixed with beach-combers, jeeps and muscle cars waited with us to park.

The party was in the home of a movie producer who lived at the foot of Beverly Glen Canyon. It was a large property with a high stone wall and a perfectly manicured yard. The house itself was huge, in the Tudor style, but the party was in the yard and the pool house. There were about a hundred and fifty people there and drugs and alcohol flowed freely. There was a table in the pool house, next to the bar, that held an assortment of drugs, being reigned over by a self-appointed "mood coordinator." Pre-rolled joints, various pills, and chunks of cocaine filled bowls laid out like condiments at a buffet. Most of the bodies in the pool were naked, and many others were casually dressed or wearing towels and wet hair from the pool.

It turned out I knew a few people at the party. The first to greet us was an actress I had dated in New York who had moved to L.A. to work in the movies. Adriana made a big show of saying hello to me, I imagine in hopes of intimidating my date.

"What a surprise to see you, darling!" She played the game well. Adriana acted as though she were already a star, and with her good looks I was sure she could be. Her stumbling block on her path to success showed in her constant sniffling. She was heavily addicted to cocaine and I gave her the same chances of becoming a famous actress as her becoming a coke whore. While engaged in the industry drivel that serves as conversation in Tinseltown, I was accosted by my old friend Jeff.

Jeff was a director of photography who had put himself through NYU Film School selling weed. Adriana, realizing she was no longer the center of attention, took the cue and walked away.

"Dude, what's up?" cried Jeff in his usual enthusiastic tone. "What are you doing in L.A.? You staying long? You gotta check out my digs. I am living on a boat down in Marina Del Rey. You gotta stop by. And who is this beautiful lady?"

I introduced Jeff to Rene as I lit a joint and passed it around. We were probably the only ones there who were not getting steadily coked up, and the only ones without drinks in our hands. I never really liked coke, but my hand felt light without a drink, so I offered to get us a round. I arrived at the bar just as Adriana was doing a huge line at the drug table. She caught my eye as she finished and approached me.

"Who's the earth muffin?" To Adriana, anyone who wasn't incredibly chic and in the film business was a lower life form.

"Just a friend."

"Then she won't mind me fucking your brains out? All the rest of these fiends will probably end up doing so much coke they won't be able to get hard."

Adriana was a freak. A natural exhibitionist, cocaine pushed her to new heights in her willingness, make that desire, to expose herself publicly. When we were dating, we had engaged in sexual conduct in all sorts of public places. It wasn't really my style, but it was hard to turn Adriana down. Hard, but I had gotten good at it after dating her. I knew it wouldn't be a stretch for her to have sex at the party, right out in the open. She was sexy, but I had been down that road before and didn't need to go back; it wasn't going to be me putting on a show with her this time.

"I'll look for you later," she said, giving my ass a little pat as she walked off.

I returned with the drinks and found Jeff and Rene deep in conversation. Rene, having noticed Adriana's body language, made a quick comment about being surprised to see me so soon.

"She's not my type."

"Anymore," Rene added, knowing I had dated her.

After a second round Rene went in search of the ladies' room, and as soon as she left Jeff announced that he was in love.

"She doesn't have too many friends out here, so I am sure she would be receptive. Now that I think of it, you guys might make quite the pair."

"I wouldn't be stepping on your toes?"

"We're just friends. I'll feel her out for you."

"Awesome!" Then Jeff got serious and said, "You probably don't know, but I am still in the biz. The movie industry is still not quite paying my bills. I hadn't really planned on staying in, but when I got out here, I met so many transplants who didn't have connections that it sort of just happened. You know, the weed you are pulling out of your pocket tastes a lot like what our host is supplying. You working out here?"

"Yes and no."

"You got a connection for me?"

"What are we talking about?"

"A few pounds per month, but if the price is right maybe a whole lot more."

"Yeah, I think I might. Let's talk tomorrow."

When Rene came back, I announced that I was going for a swim and stripped off my clothes, causing Rene to call me "nature boy" as I dove in. The pool must have had a UV filter system, because the water wasn't slimy or smelly at all. I swam a few laps and was about to get out when I felt a presence near me. I heard the theme from "Jaws" in my head as I felt a warm body press up against me. It was Adriana, who wrapped her arms around my neck, leaving me to keep her afloat.

"You are on your own; I was just getting out," I said, trying to break from her embrace.

"You wouldn't leave a woman to drown, would you?"

"I have confidence in your survival skills."

She clung to me, reminding me of old times in her sexiest voice, until I was obviously excited. She rubbed against me, but I knew she was teasing as we had always used condoms, and I was confident she wasn't thinking about having unprotected sex now. When she was sure I was getting flustered she pushed away and said, "Let's go get a drink."

"I am going to stay in for a minute. It would be a little embarrassing to get out right now."

"Suit yourself, but that is nothing to be embarrassed about."

When I finally got out of the pool, I grabbed a towel and rejoined Jeff and Rene, who were sitting poolside, engrossed in an animated conversation. As we sat there, Simon and Sebrina showed up. Simon's maxim was a little poem he had once shared with me:

"Show up late, look great, have a smashing date."

He certainly lived up to it on this occasion. In fact, with Sebrina on his arm, he would have looked great in a sweat suit. I introduced everybody and we had our own little party. Simon drifted off every now and again, but the rest of us stayed camped out on the patio loungers that were poolside until sunrise. There were two points when the rest of the party interrupted our little party. One was when Adriana and another attention-starved actress did a 69 on the diving board, and the other was breakfast. At sunrise we were momentarily invaded by an army of caterers, who laid out an awesome buffet and then disappeared as quickly as they had arrived. Half of the party continued doing lines and the rest of us dove into the awesome spread. Adriana was nowhere to be seen at this point, and I was glad to be rid of her.

When we left at seven-thirty, only about thirty people had left and the rest were either still partying or passed out somewhere. I made plans to meet Jeff later in the afternoon and left him watching Rene get into my car. We were both exhausted, so Rene decided to stay with me at the Hilton, which was only a few minutes away. She offered to sleep on the couch, but when I pointed out that the other side of the king-sized bed was as far away as the couch, we both passed out on the bed.

The morning started late and I drove her home around two in the afternoon. She asked a lot of questions about Jeff on the way. I gave him a good rating and told her that he was also interested. After answering all her questions she was satisfied and asked me to give him her phone number. I dropped her off at her house and she thanked me for taking her out.

“I knew parties like that go on every day, but was beginning to wonder if I'd ever see one. Anytime you need a date don't hesitate to call me.”

Avoiding the freeway I drove south to the Marina. I found the boat Jeff lived on and climbed aboard. He was still asleep when I found him in the cabin. His first words when he opened his eyes were, “I dreamed I met an angel last night.”

“She likes you too; here's her phone number.”

He got out of bed like a kid on Christmas morning. He assured me that I was the best friend a guy could hope for. He asked more about her and what I had told her about him.

“I left some mystery, but I did tell her you are in the biz. It was a tough spot, so I chose honesty.”

“What did she say about it?”

“She wasn't thrilled, but she also wasn't surprised. She knows what I do, so it doesn't shock her. Besides, she would be happy with a date right now; I don't think she is looking for a husband. She'll take the good with the bad. If she gets hooked, I have full confidence that she will maul you into her idea of a perfect partner and you will love the pain."

"What about a connection?"

"You met him last night, and he has agreed to work with you. We are meeting him in an hour."

"Is it the weed we were smoking last night?"

"And the weed we'll be smoking as soon as you get out of the shower."

"Dude, I love you. You show up and in twenty-four hours give my personal life and my business a boost. I am going to put you in my first feature film."

"Thanks," I said sarcastically. "For now just put a move on."

The meeting went smoothly. Simon wasn't looking for new customers, but he had taken a liking to Jeff at the party. They were the same age, a few years older than me, but while Jeff still acted like a teenager, Simon was more sophisticated and serious. I knew they would work well together and Simon would smooth Jeff's rough edges. Leaving them together at the cafe I went to try to get my money's worth out of the bed at the Hilton. After ordering room service, I slept from eight that night until eight the next morning.

After breakfast I hit the road, heading north. I decided to keep the rental car and drive so I could see the sights. It would be at least a ten-hour drive, but I wanted to see the scenery and the Volvo was comfortable. I had brought some tapes and the car's Blaupunkt stereo rocked, so I looked forward to a nice long ride.

Chapter Seven

Though it was disappointing not to have time to get out of the car and walk around, it was a beautiful drive. Highway 101 from L.A. to San Francisco offers an overview of the impressive variety of landscapes that exist in California. The sea breeze rolling over the coastal mountains kept the air crisp and exhilarating, and the irrigated farms released rich scents of every kind of produce. The sky was clear and bright the whole way, but crossing over the Golden Gate I could see the fog bank in the distance that would roll in from the ocean and envelop the city by the end of the day.

I arrived in Garberville around nine o'clock and got a room just off the freeway. After a shower, I headed over to the restaurant where the meeting had been held on my previous visit. Rose directed me to sit at the bar and somebody would tell Freedom that I was there. Sure enough, a half hour later, the gentle giant walked in. The last diners were just leaving and a few groups stood drinking at the bar. Freedom ordered a pitcher of Anchor Steam Ale and directed me to a table by the window. He was finished with his first beer and poured a second before either of us spoke. He seemed to be in a quiet mood, but after he finished his beer his expression changed and he became jovial.

"I guess this promotion means we lose one of our best trimmers?"

"If you call this a promotion, I guess I can make referrals now. I have a few people in mind who could take my place."

"One step at a time. First, we have to finish out this season. Where's your truck?"

"It will be here around one o'clock. I am going to meet the driver at a little market on the edge of town; it's the last stop on his route."

I told him about the juice truck and asked where they had decided to load the truck.

"Looks like we have a cosmic confluence going on. When we were trying to decide where would be best to back up a truck, we figured a store might be most inconspicuous. It's already at the loading dock of the store where you are meeting your driver."

"How much is there?"

"Eleven hundred pounds."

"Perfect."

"How much money did you bring?"

"1.3 mil. Rose said this goes to you guys in cash, but from now on we will make deposits into your accounts. You divide it up this time, but for my next trip out I will need you to tell me whose accounts get how much. First names only. I guess you can give that to me now."

"That'll work. We can use the money we have buried to buy from other growers. If we can find the money," he said with a smile. "We should have five to 10 thousand pounds for you this year. We'll keep you posted if we can get more."

"Excellent. I should be able to make a trip every three or four weeks. You cool with storing it that long?"

"Yeah. Actually, we feel best that way, at least until this thing develops a little further."

"Good, we'll work however you guys are most comfortable."

Freedom leaned back in his chair and took a long pull from his beer, draining his glass. As he poured us another round, I could tell he was contemplating how to say what was on his mind. He and I had become close when I worked for him and he knew I had a lot of respect for him. He finally decided on a direct approach.

"What do you know about what you are involved with here?"

"Which part?"

“The big picture.”

For a second I considered letting him believe that I knew more than I could tell him. Then I remembered his piercing ability to sense the truth and decided to be honest.

“Except for knowing the name of the contact at the bank, I haven't been told any more than they told you guys at the meeting. In fact, that was the first I had heard about it. I think they wanted someone they could trust and who wouldn't ask too many questions. Rose has always been a little secretive, so I haven't really thought about it.”

“Maybe you should.”

“The way I see it, every person, at any station in life, is the object of somebody else's direction or at least beholden to another individual or faction. Because of all this interdependency, someone is always making choices that affect our reality, so why worry about what is not in front of you? I trust Rose and Nathan, and as Justin said, there is obviously some grand plan, and if they don't want me to know all the details, I don't really care. As long as no one gets hurt and I can make money, I don't think it is important that I know.”

He considered my reasoning and didn't speak for some time. I left him to his thoughts and lit a smoke. I examined the picture on the pack of Camel non-filters and waited for his next comment.

“I guess they made a good choice in you. I'm not knocking you; you have a healthy attitude considering they would only tell you so much anyway. I thought you might know more than they told us.”

“Nathan did mention a golf date with a bank executive and a state banking auditor involving the bank where the deposits will be made.”

“Well, that's probably the tip of the iceberg. My guess is there is more to it than one bank. Nathan mentioned no helicopters next year. That is big.”

It dawned on me that I had been sucked into a current and was flowing with it. A big part of living the life of an outlaw has always been the need to be in control of my own life. I didn't want to be told what to do, or show up for some mind-numbing job five days a week, I wanted to live my own life. Selling weed has allowed me to follow my own muses and do as I please. But now most of my schedule was determined by a plan with a lot of moving parts that I didn't control.

"What do you think?" I asked.

Before he could answer the waitress brought us the check and said she was off for the night. Freedom didn't seem in a rush to answer my question, so I quietly drank my beer as I waited. The silence was suddenly unnerving.

A bit of vertigo washed over me as I wondered what my friends from high school would think about what I was doing. I had a body rush of paranoia as I contemplated what I was into for the first time. The romance and bravado dissipated as I considered what sort of trouble I would face if things came undone. Prison would certainly clip my wings.

Most of the lights were off now and we sat in the dim light until Freedom spoke up.

"Thesis plus antithesis equals synthesis."

"Come again, Professor."

Freedom smiled. He had a warm, open smile. I had called him Professor for the first time years ago. After trimming some nights, we would sit outside and he would launch into monologues equal to the greatest philosophical dissertations. He knew my addressing him as Professor was an invitation for such a speech. He pulled a joint out of his pocket, and lighting it he began his elocution.

"The goal of the aforementioned equation," he started with an aristocratic, British accent before returning to his normal, animated voice, "is change. There are people and groups who will use the tension of opposing views to create change that settles at some point of mutual dissatisfaction.

People enjoy escaping through drugs -thesis, drugs are bad -antithesis, so the politics can synthesize anywhere in the middle."

"Sorry, Prof, you lost me."

"A simple example would be a polluter donating money to an organization that espouses the highest environmental standard. Of course, the highest standard is what we all would want, but the conversation creates tension that allows the polluter to meet us tree-huggers halfway and satisfy the public."

"Do you think there is some grand plan, or is it a free for all?" I asked.

"No single group ever attains enough power to completely make over society in their interest, and we must hope that continues to be the case. The formula is a socio-political construct but, as any action requires financing, it is often played out in the realm of money. Political, social, military, and even religious motives maintain a relationship with capital. The success of the Catholic Church is in no small way related to its ability to maintain and grow its financial resources.

"In the same way that politics serves capital as a vehicle, capital serves politics. The funding of the Mujaheddin that fought against the Russian invasion of Afghanistan came from the drug trade. The CIA, anxious to find funds to support a war that most Americans hadn't even heard about, much less cared about, were willing partners in this operation that allowed the freedom fighters to buy weapons to combat the Russians."

"I remember that," I said. "We called it the hash years. I sold a bunch of kilo bricks in '84 and '85 that were stamped in gold with the emblem 'Smoke Russia Away, Free Afghanistan Now.' They were beautiful, wrapped in red crinkly plastic with the seal."

"And interestingly enough, during those years the border

with Mexico tightened so people were forced to smoke more hash instead. The actions we are supporting in El Salvador and Nicaragua are being funded by the cocaine trade. Funny how during the height of the war on drugs, the price of coke is a third of what it used to be and demand has never been higher. Tension; it all comes down to tension."

"What does all that have to do with us?"

Freedom shrugged. "Banks, stocks, no helicopters, Nathan...There must be some real power players in on this. People are not about to stop smoking pot and there is a lot of money out there, it makes sense that bigger players are getting involved."

"I guess we will know more when we find out which stocks you are buying."

"As long as it's not military industrial complex shit, we will take the ride."

"You pull out otherwise?"

"Absolutely."

It was getting late and I was tired. To move things along, I asked him if he wanted the cash now.

"Yeah, we'll count the bodies in the office."

Counting the bodies meant counting the $5000 bundles. It would have taken a couple of people most of the night to actually count it all. I grabbed my suitcase and we went into the office.

"258, 259, 260 times $5000," he said, grabbing a calculator. "Looks good. Ask for my brother when the truck comes in. it is all boxed up and waiting in the shipping area of the store, twenty-two pounds per box, fifty boxes."

We left the restaurant and Freedom locked up. He never mentioned owning the place, and I figured even if he didn't own it, whoever did wouldn't hesitate to give him the keys. As I left him, I told him Rose would be in touch when I was on my way back.

After a peaceful night in the motel, I wandered around the

redwoods to kill time before meeting the truck. At one o'clock I pulled into the market's parking lot right behind the juice truck. The driver was a cheerful Vietnam vet named Pat who had been a friend of my parents when they were in college. My dad had kids, which kept him from being drafted, but Pat was not so lucky. After the destruction he saw on his first tour he had no choice but to submerge himself in the nightmare and he did two more. He had spent a total of four-and-a-half years, gun in hand, in the confusion that was Vietnam.

He was a cool customer and didn't flinch when he saw how many boxes we put on his truck. He didn't know what he was carrying. It was an easy assumption, but I had asked him not to ask and he was getting well paid for his discretion. When the door closed, I slapped a padlock on the truck and clicked it shut. Pat looked disappointed.

"It's not for you. If you wanted to get inside, I am sure a padlock wouldn't slow you down. It's for the random chance someone tries to open it at a traffic light or a rest stop. What a bonus that would be for the person hoping to steal a case of juice. I'll beat you down there and will be waiting at the dock."

I wondered if I should tell him about Nathan's insurance policy. Nathan trusted me about the driver, and had probably checked him out, but he wanted some security against the black hole of the law. Apparently, whoever was going to tail the truck would be able to pull rank on any officer that might happen to pull the truck over. I didn't want Pat to get nervous if he spotted the tail so I told him.

"By the way, some friends in high places wanted to make sure that you had a safe trip. You will have a shadow during your drive."

"Ain't that special," he said, sure that he wasn't being trusted.

"That shadow will be a get-out-of-jail-free card."

"Now, that is special," he said, pleased that his integrity

was not in question.

"Have a nice drive," I said and headed toward my car.

I got to the industrial park in South San Francisco just before six o'clock and found my cousin Carla on a lounge chair in an open bay of the dock, reading Dostoevsky.

"Hey, Cuz. Have a smooth trip?"

"Fast and smooth. And how are you?"

"Same. Fast and smooth."

We talked for a while until Pat showed up with the truck around seven. We unloaded the boxes and left them on the loading dock for the night. We would come back in the morning to crate them up. The weekend crowds were gearing up to release another week's worth of tension, but I wasn't in the party spirit. I suggested to my cousin that we just hang out at her place and drink some wine while we caught up with each other's lives and family gossip. We ordered some Thai food and sat up late into the night drinking some Sonoma Pinot Noir, and reminiscing about our wacky family members.

Her mother, my aunt, had recently married a gentleman who communicated with aliens via his left thumb. He was pretty harmless when he was on his meds, but when he got off them it became surreal. Once the medication wore off, he became an ambassador for humanity who was the vehicle for the extra-terrestrial communications being sent to pave the way for the arrival of pilgrims from space. I really wanted to know what they were saying, but apparently curiosity or indulgence on another's part was known to push him over the edge. I like looking over edges, but never had a chance to understand what he was looking at.

I guess every family has a few loose screws. We might have had more than a few. Carla and I laughed at each other for carrying such genetic material and happily agreed we were unscrewed as well.

In the morning we drove back down to the dock and

packed the boxes into crates. Each crate held eighteen boxes. I sent the two complete crates to New York and the one with only fourteen boxes to L.A. The shipment would take three days to L.A. and five to New York. This meant that the load wouldn't reach the receiving department in New York until the following Tuesday. I figured I could spend the rest of the weekend with my cousin and then head down to Santa Cruz to hang with Karen for a few days and still be back east in time to receive the load.

My cousin was psyched; both she and Pat were making $10,000 per trip and she insisted on taking me out to a big dinner to celebrate her first paycheck. We went to a small French Vietnamese spot that she really liked and ate and drank until the restaurant closed. After dinner we walked back to her place. The fog had rolled in and the town took on the mood of an English murder mystery film. It wasn't a long walk, but our full bellies weighed us down and when we arrived at her house, we both plopped ourselves down and only moved to pass the joints for the next few hours.

"What do you want?" Carla asked me.

"I want a lot of things," I said.

"Ah, things. That is the problem right there. We are all so wrapped up in our things we don't see each other, or nature, or what is happening in front of us. We judge and are judged by our things. How many, how cool, how rare or expensive? Wealth should be measured by the depth of experience."

"That is closer to what I meant by wanting a lot of things. Not stuff. I grew up in a small apartment and have always disliked clutter. I would like to be a carpenter, a sailor, a painter, a musician, a scientist, a politician…well, maybe not a politician. The problem is it takes a lifetime to do any of those things well and that means you only do one thing in a lifetime. Sometimes I feel so overwhelmed with the choices I fear I will miss the opportunity to do any of them."

"I guess no matter what you do, it is the way you do it that matters. Right now I am going to sleep, and plan on doing it well."

With that, Carla went off to sleep and I passed out in the lazy boy.

Still in a fog of sleep, I called Karen in the morning to see if she had time to hang. She told me that she had been thinking of me and would love to see me. She gave me directions to her place and by mid-afternoon I was sitting on her deck with a view of the ocean. She lived in a tipi a few miles from the coast in a valley called Trout Gulch. The hills outside Santa Cruz are one of the few places where one can grow both orange and apple trees and her front yard was an Eden of tree-ripened fruit. The yard area was a bit rough except for a border around the tipi where there were flowers and grass that looked manicured. Even the fruit trees weren't planted in any order and the grasses around them did their own thing, mostly looking shaggy.

I had never been in a big tipi before. It was probably 25 feet in diameter and even though the walls closed in, there was a feeling of space. She had worked to keep hard angles from intruding on the organic feel of the tipi and none of her furniture was square. The counters had rounded corners; the couch must have come out of a cabaret because it was arc shaped. Soft corners and soft lighting made it feel like being in a genie bottle.

Within minutes of my arrival we were both undressed and greedily making up for lost time. With no neighbors, there was no concern making love on her deck. After working a few postures and Karen arriving at a place where I felt I could slow down, I entered her from behind while standing. I tried to time my rhythm with the sound of the ocean which, though it was miles away, could still be heard. Slow, in and out. An eagle was catching a draft in the sunshine and we paused and discussed its grace and freedom.

"Come on, let's go inside and finish this on my bed."

I hadn't noticed before, but her bed was circular as well, and all the pillows were leaning against each other in the center of the bed. Sometimes on a king-sized bed I don't know which way to lie, but on a circular bed there were no cues at all. It didn't matter while we made love, but later when we went to sleep it was confusing without a straight line to align myself with.

Karen stayed present when making love. Her eyes were open 99% of the time. Only when she climaxed did they close for a brief moment before opening again with that deep calm she always seemed to carry. Making love to her was like a long massage that happened to have genitalia involved. Sometimes my eyes would close as I drifted off into some film roll of past and imagined entanglement of body parts and she would gently but insistently bring me back to her, and those eyes. I can't even say what color her eyes were. They had poppy field explosions that seemed to change hue with no trigger. You couldn't focus on the color anyway because when you looked in her eyes you didn't see her eyes, you saw soul, history, capital W woman.. A deep well that went to the reverse of a black hole, not sucking mass but spewing love.

I think the thing that amazed me most about Karen is she didn't talk about esoteric stuff. She didn't have a rap about how she lived or loved, she just did it, with a presence not born of intellectual striving or meticulous practice, but birthed with her as she arrived on this earth and stepped into the rain of grace that molded her exquisite spirit. She was vegetarian, she meditated, grew a lot of her own food, was involved in a local group that helped old folks manage. She was a runner and swimmer and did it all without insisting anyone else notice what she was up to. She cared deeply for people, people in general, but she didn't pass judgment or preach, or bother to explain her own choices unless asked.

When we were done she handed me a guitar and said, "Play for me". She was asleep when I put the guitar down.

Chapter Eight

I headed back to L.A. on Saturday to catch my flight back to New York. After spending the week with Karen, I took the slow route along the coast back to L.A. Once past Vandenberg Air Force Base I left the two-lane state highway and entered the chaos of the Ventura Freeway. The traffic and the smog of the San Fernando Valley jolted me out of the relaxed state I had assumed in the Santa Cruz hills. Karen lived a life that was mostly barefoot, filled with organic produce and good air, and was more relaxed than my New York state-of-mind could fathom. It was something so beautiful and simple I couldn't conceive it even when I was in it. Life didn't seem real without the clutter and rush of metro-crazed activity.

After being cut off a few times by impatient drivers, I left my laid-back self behind and re-assumed the frantic pace of twentieth century cosmopolitan living. I tried to picture Karen in New York City and realized that she would be totally out of place. There was no place for the lifestyle she had carved out for herself among the psychotically driven masses that negotiated their survival among the glass and steel monoliths that dominate city life.

I smoked a joint just before I returned the rental car and glided into the terminal with just enough time to board the plane before takeoff. Once in my seat I put my sunglasses on, earplugs in, and informed the stewardess that it was my intent to sleep through the entire flight back east. I was out before takeoff and awoke during the approach to Newark Airport. Six in the morning in the city leaves few options. I could go home, catch an early church service, or go to an after-hours club. I knew some of my friends would be at Save the Robots on the Lower East Side and the party would be in high gear. Since I only had a small backpack I used as a carry-on, I decided to go straight to the club. Even though I had slept on the plane, I still felt as if I had been up all night, and since California time was three hours earlier it felt natural to step into a late-night scene.

I hadn't been there a half hour when I saw Kiki. He was my age and had connections for Mexican that were as good as mine, but he had a bigger market. He worked with some "family" types who were also into powders, prostitution, gambling, and garbage. He managed his affairs well and maintained good relations with his connections. I always warned him about working with the mob, to which he would always respond that the mafia doesn't exist. Because we could get similar prices we rarely worked together, but we got together every few months to compare notes.

"Damn, that smells good," he said, smelling the joint I was smoking. Cocaine was rampant in the club and there were few takers when I offered to share my joint, but Kiki doesn't do powders and is one of the few people who can smoke as much weed as I do.

"You know me, nothing but the best."

"I am still smoking from the two pounds I bought from you last spring, but I'm almost out. I'd hate to have to smoke what I sell," he said with a smile. "You got any more of this?"

"As much as you want."

"Really? The last time I bought some high-end you told me the price went up if I wanted more."

"Supply and demand, my friend. That was then and this is now. I can get a lot more now."

"I'll take it all."

"Slow down, you might be in over your head."

"You got some I can look at?"

"Just a little under an ounce on me." I threw the bag on the table. The freshly trimmed buds were bursting with California sunshine.

"This looks great, how much can I get?"

"Don't you want to know the price?"

"It almost doesn't matter, but yeah, how much?"

"$3500 a pound."

"Can I get fifty?"

"Sure, it should be in by mid-week. I'll call you on Wednesday."

The party was winding down around ten am, so I split and walked back to the west side. My apartment has southern exposure, and in the spring and fall the sun pours through the large windows. I had only spent four nights at home in the last six weeks, and it felt good to be surrounded by my own stuff. Even though I hadn't been there, my housekeeper still came in once a week and the place was immaculate and all my plants looked healthy. I plopped into my big comfortable chair and inhaled the essence of home. I thought about what the man on the plane had said about people who had to travel a lot. I knew in the months to come, I would be spending as much time in hotel rooms as I would at home.

I paged Rose around noon, and we made plans to meet at one pm. There was an exhibit of Monet at the Met and she had tickets and wanted me to go with her. We cabbed it uptown and were quickly absorbed by the weekend museum crowd. With her arm through mine we toured the wonderful pieces whose subject was mainly the artist's residence at Giverny. Monet's style is almost more intelligible from a distance through squinted eyes. There wasn't the usual problem of people crowding near the pieces, because up close there were only brushstrokes visible. Rose informed me that not only did Monet paint the paintings, but he also designed the gardens so he could paint them. Scores of maintenance workers planted over one-hundred and fifty thousand plants each year to develop his vision.

Only after we made the rounds of Monet did we talk business.

"So your trip went well?"

"Very well. My friend in L.A. had more cash than I had expected. I gave Freedom 1.3 million. There are 792 pounds that will be here tomorrow and 308 in L.A. already, so right now we owe 2.3 million. I paid my cousin and the driver and everyone is ready for the next trip. Freedom said we should expect five to ten thousand pounds this year."

"What was Freedom's vibe?"

"He seemed comfortable with how things were looking. He mentioned that they felt better keeping the stock out there until they see how things are working out. All the growers are digging up their cash reserves and trying to buy up lots from their neighbors and hope to have even more than ten thousand pounds. I guess that shows confidence in the investment plan. He did share some lengthy conjecture about the politics of the grand plan."

"Like what?"

"Some equation; I think it was thesis plus antithesis equals synthesis and how capital serves its own ends. That dude can get pretty macro when he wants."

"Well, to be honest, Nathan hasn't shared that much with me. I know the goal of raising capital is to invest in personal computing technology. Some of the people involved are people I know from the old days, but I can't be sure we have the same goals."

"What are your goals? Besides making a bunch of money, of course."

"I think that if we can make computers that everyone can afford, and find a way to connect them into large networks, we can spawn the biggest democratic revolution since the Bill of Rights."

"How is that?"

"It comes down to access. Authority, as it currently exists, acts as a gatekeeper maintaining control over access to information. If we can democratize access to information, the next stage of social evolution will increase our experience of freedom."

"Somehow that doesn't seem like Nathan's thinking."

"His motivation probably has a more nationalistic nature, and is undoubtedly involved in a manipulation of the way wealth is focused in the world. But I have to tell you even though I have known him for 20 years, I still don't have him pegged."

"His and your motivations seem mutually exclusive."

"The final goals might be, but the means are the same. Once there is a dynamic of change unleashed, it is not so easily directed. I believe there is a steady progression toward empowerment of the individual that is revealed historically and will continue to be the determining force in the future."

"Your optimism is one of the many things that make you so beautiful."

She gave me a kiss on the cheek for the compliment.

We left the museum and headed back downtown. Rose told me that Nathan would be at the Receiving Department to meet the load with me, and to hear about the trip. She asked me to bring up a box or two to her apartment after we were finished unloading. The delivery service was already busy and both she and I had a lot of orders. From the way Rose talked and what I knew I could sell, I was sure I would be on my way back out west in two or three weeks.

I spent the rest of the day at home. I caught up on some bills and made a bunch of phone calls that I had neglected for weeks. Many were social, but since the marijuana trade was at the center of my social life, most of the calls also involved business.

The receiving department was one of the few single-story buildings in Lower Manhattan. We were the only tenant in the three-thousand-square-foot building and the rent was $4000 per month. The previous tenant had been a welder who had gotten carried away with security concerns and had welded the building into a veritable fortress. The only entrance was through the front, which was a series of huge metal doors that a tank would have had trouble piercing. There was an office area in the front and the entire rest was open space. Nathan had installed a couple of large freezers to store the buds and keep them in good shape.

"What do you think about some sort of sign?" he asked when I arrived. "Our neighbors might wonder what is going on in here."

"The block isn't very busy, and you know New Yorkers are not very nosy. I think it will look like what it is, storage. The less we put out there, the better."

"We should have some cover in mind so we have congruent stories for the occasional inquisition. Since the boxes come marked as medical supplies, we should follow that line."

"How about chiropractic supplies? Chiropractic is out of the mainstream and we can deflect questioning with new-age psycho-babble about holistic healing."

"You should have been in advertising; chiropractic supplies it is."

We were there for an hour when the truck arrived. The delivery was made by a local trucking company that received it from the transcontinental shipper. The driver was very businesslike and had us sign the receipt when the two crates were on the sidewalk. He drove away as Nathan appeared with a pallet jack to bring the crates inside. We moved them right to the back and began filling the freezers. Nathan had already developed a system to keep track of the inventory. There was a clipboard with forms on which we would write dates and amounts when we took product out.

Nathan gave me more direction. "We should leave them in the boxes and move them around twenty-two pounds at a time. Since it is so close to the messenger service and both yours and Rose's apartments, you can make frequent trips as needed. You can easily carry two boxes at a time to the corner, where there is never a problem catching a cab. I'll get some twine and handles to tie to the boxes, which should make it easier and look more professional. You should try to keep your visits here to business hours to avoid suspicion. Also, you should always dress in business clothes, casual if you want, but let's keep up the facade by staying squeaky clean."

When we had all but two boxes in the freezers, he asked about my trip. I gave him the details and assured him that everything had gone smoothly. I decided against telling him about Freedom's dissertation, thinking it would be better if Nathan didn't know a conversation about motives was being held. I would rather he think I had never considered a bigger picture.

I left Nathan and headed uptown with the two boxes. He stayed behind to finish making the front of the space into a more believable office and to gather supplies to make the operation run smoothly. He was going to have a phone line installed so the shipping company would have a number to call, and so he could use it as a part-time office. Apparently, the weed business wasn't the only activity he wanted to hide from his partners at the law firm, where he had a lavish office. There was no missing the mysterious nature of his thinking, and I couldn't help but wonder how many balls he was juggling.

I stopped at Rose's apartment and dropped off one of the boxes. She said she would need at least two more for the next day and asked if I could bring them by before noon. She hoped I would have time as she was going to be very busy. In the future she would have no problem going downtown for herself. I asked her what was in it for me. She recognized my tone and suggested that if I was there by ten, we would have a little time for some fun. Although I was dating a few girls my own age, I was hooked on Rose. It wasn't a romantic addiction or a narcotizing lust, she was simply the best sexual partner I had ever experienced. There was no doubt I would be there by ten.

"What's your demand look like?" she asked.

"Could be as much as a hundred pounds per week, maybe more. There seems to be a greatly increasing demand."

"Here too. My only concern is I would like to keep the delivery service going year-round. I think it will end up being ten to twenty pounds per week. Obviously, we have the greatest mark-up on retail, which helps offset expenses, so we should make sure we set enough aside to get us through the summer."

"Sounds like six hundred pounds or so."

"Which means we will have to put the brakes on the wholesale business when we start getting low."

"I'm game, what about Nathan?"

"He'll go along with it."

"Cool, I got to go. I'll see you in the morning."

I took my box home and hadn't been there a half hour when the phone started ringing. The first few visitors took four and five pounds each, so by three o'clock, I started scheduling people for the next day. Although I was referring most of my smaller customers to the delivery service, there were still a few friends that I sold ounces and quarter pounds. By evening there had been twenty customers through my apartment and the whole building smelled of kind bud, so much so that my downstairs neighbors knocked on my door hoping to catch a buzz. They were an older gay couple who were part of the Village scene in the '60s and some of the few remaining members of Andy Warhol's clique. They were great people and broke most of the time, so after hanging out for an hour I threw them an ounce when they left.

The next morning I was at Rose's at nine-thirty with three boxes and a hard-on. When she chased me out at twelve-thirty, I was exhausted and went home and took a very peaceful daytime nap.

Chapter Nine

I awoke to the phone ringing. In fact, it rang all afternoon. The conversations were mostly social, but would include a time to meet at my house. I figured the cops weren't interested in busting weed dealers, but was still cautious and never discussed amounts or used any sort of code on the phone. My clients knew that if I didn't have what they wanted, I wouldn't make plans to see them. This method had always worked well with the Mex, because I knew what most of my customers wanted. With the kind bud being a new market it was going to be a little trickier, but I would make up for it by always having plenty on hand. I figured that if I couldn't fill an order they could always come back the next day. This ended up happening quite often as everybody wanted more than I expected.

Rose had a lot of social connections and was always getting me invited to parties to advertise the delivery service. It was a cakewalk. All I had to do was light a few joints and hand out business cards. Many of the parties were attended by artists, actors, writers and the monied types who support the arts. Most people were still doing coke, but it wasn't like the early '80s when people did lines on tables, bars, or the back of their hand in the middle of a crowd. This was the era of squeezing into the bathroom stall. Even though the drugs were getting steadily cheaper and most people still did coke, nobody shared or admitted doing it. I was thankful for one of cocaine's most annoying effects: people who do coke want to talk, usually about some deeply personal issues that are not party conversation. Not being a user put me in demand because I was willing to listen. There is no better way to make friends than listening.

At one such party Rose told me to expect to meet a man

named Garrett and I should try to make a good impression. She would try to make it later in the evening, but I should arrive by 9. She also told me that most of the people at the party were in the biz; many knew each other socially without realizing they were in the same industry. The party was filled with fashionable hippies. There were a few people I had met in Holland, a few Deadheads from California and an older woman who was responsible for the "family export business" in Hawaii. I had popped a couple of tabs and had settled into a cozy groove by the time I got to the party and my smile, and the joints I lit, were an open invitation. There were a lot of cigarette smokers at the party and I felt I had to fight my way through the smoke that furled like impenetrable iron. As I made my way through the room, I overheard a conversation that threaded through the small group. Anyone who has never had a psychedelic experience may not understand, but sometimes as you pass through a room you hear one word from one person and a phrase from the next, and laughter from over there, all unrelated, and meanwhile your brain mends it together as one conversation, one thought even. This was occurring and I heard, "he'sbronxscience I knowabouthim metatthegreeks'83 trusthimlikeFAMILY understandstheplan thoughdoesn'tknowanylyrics, seemstoknoweverybody." Then the dimensions of the room churned Escher-like as I negotiated seating on the couch.

Trying to understand the meaning behind this clandestine grouping, I was snapped alert by a well-manicured hand thrust at me that led from some tennis player forearms to a Lacoste shirt sleeve to a cleanly shaven face. I felt better. This guy was out of place too. Bill, an older hippie from San Fran, piped up, "Hey, have you met Garrett? His dad was a pioneer in selling grass, a regular Joe Kennedy of marijuana. Dad was smart enough to send him to conservative schools so we would always know the other side." It turned out that Garrett was central in introducing me to a whole new clientele, mostly stockbrokers. Trying to stay in touch with the conversation through the barrage of patchouli, pot smoke and Santana I didn't grasp most of the conversation so kept nodding my head with as wise a face as I could muster at 22 years old, which led this “committee” to feel I was cool-headed and together.

There were many other people at the party I was given seemingly special introductions to, all of whom received business cards. I was on a mission, but with the acid in high gear and a few drinks in me I was overcome with a need to cuddle, and ended up greeting everyone with the same ecstatic pedantic. Finally finding a safe haven, I fell into the arms of a Cali girl named Meadow. It was hard to know whether Meadow was 19 or 49; she had an innocent face with ancient eyes that made me feel like Sir Lancelot from the first time my eyes met hers. My trip took an interesting turn as my mind interpreted the hippie garb as old world costumes. Everyone’s voice took on a British, Robin Hood air and I spent the rest of the evening babbling, trying to draw players into the medieval plot quickly developing in my head. I think Meadow played a key role in making sure I was seen as comedic and not lunatic.

I awoke the following morning to a ringing phone. I could usually answer and have a conversation without ever losing sleep. But this morning was different. Garrett's voice seemed insistent so I was awake with a start. "Meet me at the cafe that always plays Duran Duran," and then a dial tone. This was weird, I had only met the guy the night before and here he was calling my phone, whose number I hadn't relayed, making secretive meetings, all with a voice of authority. I figured somebody must have had trouble. In such a tight knit circle there were so few busts that word spread quickly and sometimes came from outside sources. Then I realized I had no idea where he was talking about. In the shower I ran it over and over in my head. Who still plays Duran Duran? I was thinking who I might call to ask about Garrett's strange message. Not knowing who might be in trouble, or if there was trouble at all, I was stymied.

Randomly I thought of Randy, the seller in the Village who had initiated me to magic at a pentangle on the old West Side Highway when I was 15. He had given three of us mushrooms and told us we were going to watch the procession of the gods. It was summer solstice eve and we went for a walk and "stumbled" upon this pentangle spray painted on the road. The elevated roadway had been closed for years and was generally used as a recreation area. Sure enough, after he had us lie in the circle one at a time and danced and sang incantations while doing a swirling dance, at sunrise there was a string of clouds that as he pointed them out became easily recognizable. Apollo and his chariot leading the way, it blended into a beautiful parade of gods and idols from many cultures. There were Hindu gods and Greek gods and ancient idols. I tried to note the order and pairings so I could make sense of it later, but afterwards I couldn't remember. It had all blended into a feeling.

Somewhere in this recollection I remembered having last seen Randy in a coffee shop on the east side. In the midst of his ranting he pointed out nobody listened to Duran Duran anymore, yet in this cafe their glory lived on. As I grabbed my jacket to leave, I wondered if Garrett and Randy knew each other. As I stepped into the sunshine, I had a weirder thought: Had Randy sent the idea? A visitation to my hallucinatory, over-responsive brain?

When I saw Garrett he was standing in front of the cafe. As he noticed me, he started to stroll away. He was walking slowly, so I easily overtook him. He made no sign that he noticed me, but he began speaking. He said he didn't want to be seen with me so we should keep walking. I had mastered the waves of paranoia that came with the business, though I still often felt like I was being watched. I figured if I stayed a small operator, I would never attract the attention of the feds and the regular police were easy enough to avoid. You would have had to drop a pound in front of them to get caught. Now Garrett walked in a store, out a fire exit that led to the next block, then went to the subway, paid our fare only to walk to the exit at the other end and into an underground coffee shop. He played a serious game. I wondered who he thought might try to follow him. He seemed like some trickster who made it look like a big deal just to get you off your guard. As usual I felt I had nothing to lose.

He told me the bad guys don't get out of their cars, to shake them I should employ the tactics he just did. Then he gave me a layman's education in surveillance and counter-surveillance. I was mostly interested in the cute waitress, but being a good student I got what he was saying. He also kept repeating that I was not a teenager anymore and it was time to take this more seriously. He said, "They take it very seriously." At the end of the conversation he handed me a floppy disc with a phone number on it.

Now, this was a 7-inch floppy, the latest. I had randomly ended up with one of the first PCs that had a hard drive when a friend's company was upgrading and of course it had a floppy disc drive. And at that time there was no WWW. anything. There were networks at colleges and banks, governmental networks, etc. To interact you had to dial a phone number for the company and log onto their system. Clunky word processing was the best you could hope for. Searches took forever and found little, but one thing that worked very well was the transmission of documents. Garrett had given me a dial-up number and an encryption program so I could communicate via a bulletin board in secrecy. That was the method I was to use for communications with all the parties involved.

When I thought we were done with our meeting, Garrett asked if I wanted to go to a museum. I found the request odd after the seriousness of our conversation, especially considering we hardly knew each other.

"I have the afternoon free and thought I would play tourist. Smoke a fatty in the park and soak up some culture?" he asked.

I am not sure what his motives really were. I guess I can't blame him if he wanted to check me out. I figured it was in my professional interests to hang with him and hear what else he might have to say.

Sitting in Sheep's Meadow we perfumed the air with the blessings of California sunshine. Garrett asked me how I got interested in the business. While I usually told the story as if I was in control of the direction my life was taking, sitting there in the sunshine in a post-bliss serotonin crash it came out with more truth than I usually reveal.

"Pretty simply, I guess. I never really made a choice to get into it. I just never made the choice not to. Some friends from high school gave me some money to buy for them in Washington Square and they would get me high. The first person I met when I went to the park was Hippy Larry, who gave me a deal so I actually made $20. I saw Hippy Larry a few days later when I was walking my dog and he made me a proposition: he would front me a quarter pound and we would split the profit. He was confident that at a high school like Bronx Science I would be able to find customers. He was right. When I had flipped my first quarter pound Larry gave me another. That is when my mom found it in my drawer. She asked me to explain what I was up to and I told her, including the fact that it had gotten me invited to some pretty cool places. She didn't smoke, but wasn't against it and was certainly clear that the laws governing marijuana were wrong. She told me if I was going to try to sell weed I should call my old babysitter who was living in Chelsea. I left Chelsea that very afternoon with a 35-pound bale fronted to me at hundreds of dollars cheaper than anyone else in town. I took it home, went back out and bought a scale on Canal Street and broke it up into pounds. I went to the park and over the next two weeks Hippy Larry introduced me to Hairy Larry, who introduced me to Crazy Larry, who introduced me to Dana and the Yippies. By the time I went to my first pot parade most of the weed in the joints the Yippies were handing out was from me. Pretty heady at 15 years old. Somewhere along the way I met Rose and now I am involved in this."

"What do you think this is?"

"What I know is that we are moving money above board in hope of accomplishing a revolution in human communication. Our success, besides making a lot of money, won't be measurable for a decade and if successful we can never take credit or talk about it. I know some of the details of the plan but have been advised to let my curiosity remain dormant about the rest."

"Well, you nailed the short view. I don't think anyone has thought past the point of success, if we are successful, very clearly yet. There is still this fascination with how machines can make our lives better and the advances in science and technology are always sold to us as improvements to our lives."

He suggested we get to the exhibit he wanted to visit and got up and started walking. When we got there, I was surprised to find that it wasn't an art exhibit; it was an exploration of some of the important documents that have shaped our political and social life over the centuries. There were some Greek and Roman texts, Brehon laws from Ireland that were probably the first written laws about religious tolerance, the Magna Carta, the Declaration of Independence and others. There was a timeline on the wall that expressed the evolution of the idea of personal liberty and notable moments in the conflict between the individual and society.

"That was the perfect setup for what I would like to share with you now," he said as we left the exhibit. "I want to tell you why I am part of this…project if you will."

"Not for the money?"

"No, I was born with enough money, I am in it for the excitement and a specific goal. Everybody working on the project is so concerned with making it successful that no one is thinking about what happens if we are successful. This new way of communicating and sharing ideas offers potential we can only dream about now, but also will easily lend itself to control and abuse by state or corporate actors. I want to be sure that whatever comes out of this is free, accessible, allows for privacy and offers something more than a sales tool for commercial interests."

"Well, that sounds utopic. What are the odds of that happening?

"On its own, not very good. But a technological problem often has a technological solution. We need to stay one step ahead and make sure, if this project is successful, we have more than a loud voice to contribute. I picture countless kids at home with a punk ethos cracking holes in whatever control mechanism the system throws at us. We are going to make sure that governments and corporations aren't able to take over the system, whether it be privacy, freedom of choice or access."

"And how are we going to do that?" I tried to not sound patronizing, but the messiah complex was thick.

"Nothing short of revolution. We are going to spawn a generation of hackers who for fun and principle will be a nuisance to anyone trying to restrict the free flow of ideas. A marketing campaign to make whistle-blowers national heroes. Support for left-wing computer science departments at universities. Basically shouting wolf until others see the wolf in the room."

"That sounds fun. What can I do to help?"

"Be an investor."

"Invest in something with no personal return?"

"Listen, it is all a dream so why not play it on your terms? If a few of us throw a few million at the problem, who knows what we can do? I can see so clearly how this amazing new technology gets choked out by commercial interests and the fearful fantasies of state players. It could be dead on arrival while being heralded as a great leap forward of humanity."

I looked at him. Crazy as it was, I was considering it. I knew he was legit and probably had a team of ivy league devotees on his payroll ready to execute his plan. I was admittedly a bit ungrounded at the time and felt guilty and awkward with the amount of money I was making. Why not give it all away? Well, not all, of course. It came easy and will continue to come easy for as long as I don't cling to it. That was how I rationalized it anyway. And in some way, I needed a final solution to get rid of all the money I was making. I stuck out my hand.

When I got home, I turned on my computer and inserted the disc. The number on the drive was an 800 number and I had no idea where I was calling but it did make communications a lot easier. I logged on as Banjo and immediately recognized the nicknames of some of the other users. I was looking at a green screen with a list of users, but there were no commands, certainly not buttons to click. I noticed there was a .txt file at the bottom where I found some basic directions that included a firm warning to update my encryption every time I logged on. Windows had come out but Garrett had serious security questions about using it for comms, so he used an early version of BBS that he had mangled some private key encryption onto. I gave it a test by writing to Robert. My message was simply, "Hot tub next weekend?"

On Tuesday I sold another fifty pounds and on Wednesday met up with Kiki to sell him his fifty. Luckily, Rose had a cash counting machine, as it would have taken a couple of hours a day just to count all the cash rolling in. The bills still had to be straightened out and faced before they were fed into the machine, but it saved a lot of time. We were selling a hundred pounds or more per day, and it was a little hectic, but with the Receiving Department only a mile cab ride away it was easy to keep up with the orders. Sometimes I could even arrange to sell twenty-two-pound lots, so I could just carry an unopened box and do the deal in my customer's car. This worked well for a lot of out-of-towners because the stash spot was right near the Holland Tunnel and they wouldn't have to worry about parking. It was easy enough to arrange to meet someone on a corner, jump in their car, take a ride to count the bodies and jump out with a bag of cash. It was easy money. There was a lot of trust in the marijuana business, so my clients never needed to look in the box. They also liked the vacuum-sealed bags that didn't emit any odors. Breaking up bales of Mex into singles or five-pound chunks was a drag, and almost impossible to pack them so they wouldn't smell. The packaging of the kind bud made it much easier to deal with, which was important because it left more time to deal with all the cash.

By the end of the second week we had gathered enough cash for me to be on my way. We still had fifty pounds to hold over a few customers and the delivery service in the freezers downtown. 2.3 million dollars filled a medium-sized suitcase to the max, and was pretty heavy. The cash was in 20s, 50s, and 100s and the suitcase weighed about a hundred and forty pounds. This was too much to carry so we ended up splitting it between three suitcases and packing the empty space with packing material. Of course we bought the best luggage to ensure that it would not break open when the baggage handlers threw the cases around.

After being in New York for only two weeks, I headed to the airport to grab a morning flight to L.A. and pick up whatever cash Simon had before heading to Sacramento. When I met Simon, he had what he owed us and a down payment on the next load. While standing in line to buy my ticket from LAX to Sacramento I considered another destination. I was twenty-two years old and had over three million dollars in my possession. I no longer had family in New York City and wasn't sure I wanted to stay there. I conjured images of a lavish life in some foreign country and let my mind run free. When the ticket agent addressed me, I popped right back into the moment. I realized I was in it for the excitement as much as the money, and bought my ticket to Sacramento.

Chapter Ten

The Wells Fargo bank in downtown Sacramento was everything a New York bank was not and lacked all the feeling of a New York bank. In New York, there had been enough money sitting around for centuries that banks had become breeding grounds for money. The air was filled with a smell, as if there was a fungus that only grew on currency. Its vapors collected as thick as church incense during mass. The tellers, legionnaires recruited for the campaign, performed their duties with all the pomp of the East Indian Company. In Sacramento, it was all different. Smiling tellers greeted customers in a modern setting without the intrusion of bulletproof glass. The building still had that new-car smell and lacked the imperious marble façade that emphasized the power of money at New York banks. It looked as if the architect had seen a picture of an East Coast bank and thought the seriousness of the construct had been a design flaw or an effect of age that needed mending. Whereas New York banks looked to be able to withstand the ravages of time, man, and nature, this bank looked as if a windstorm would threaten its very existence. To Californians, I'm sure this seemed an improvement.

Sacramento itself seemed like a massive strip mall that perhaps an earthquake had tilted a few strips vertically to twenty or thirty stories. The town had a relaxed feeling, as if someone had forgotten to tell it that it was a city. Dominated by freeways, there was a sense of a cloverleaf gone mad thinking it was a state capital. Of course it is the capital, and quite prosperous. The university presence was everywhere and all the inhabitants thrived on car culture. I had gone to a nightclub on Saturday night and it felt to me that I was in a Midwestern college town. It seemed strangely devoid of signs of flower power and the heavily marketed hippie symbols of California and felt deeply entrenched in the Reagan Republican mindset. My once-over impression was that it was square and liked it that way. I guess with L.A. and San Francisco so close, all the freaks probably migrated once they were past toddlerhood.

I left the suitcases in the trunk and went to find Robert. It was eleven o'clock and I was pleased to find him available.

"Hello, Mr. Jones," he said in a formal tone as he ushered me into his office.

"Sorry, Jones was the first name that popped in my head. Have you seen the advert that uses Grace Jones to sell Honda mini-scooters with the tag 'Keep up with the Jones'? Obviously, it is referring to jonesing for more cocaine. I can't believe that coke culture is so prevalent in American society. I saw the ad on the back of the UC Sacramento course catalogue. Man, it's good to see you, how was your trip?"

"It was fine. I got in on Saturday afternoon."

"Dude, you should've called me." In his office he slipped out of his formal tone and reverted back to his stoner dialect.

"I tried once and then got caught up exploring your fine city."

"As if. Should we do lunch?"

"Isn't it early?"

"Banker's hours. I gotta be back in time for the noon rush. You ready?"

"Unless we can smoke in your office."

"No can do. I am doing a good job of impersonating an upstanding member of conservative culture while on the premises. Probably shouldn't blow it right when the fun is starting."

He took me to a nice spot within walking distance whose name could have been the Avocado. At least half of the dishes on the menu advertised avocado and I imagined the rest probably slipped in a slice or two as a garnish.

"You going to any shows this year?"

"I'm gonna try and catch New Year's. The Tom Tom Club is opening. That should be fun. I met a girl while I was trimming this year that lives out here and she wants me to go."

"Oh yeah? A West Coast fling? She's a Head, huh? Does she shave her armpits?"

"Thank God, but she does wear a lot of patchouli. She has a law degree, but is living off the land and working as a trimmer every year. She lives in a tipi in the hills above Santa Cruz. She's really sweet and an acrobat when it comes to getting down."

"Quite a change for you. In New York I always see you with sophisticated cosmopolitan types."

"Variety is the essential spice. But I don't think it's up to me whom I date. I think it's the women who do the choosing; we just let them know if we are interested. If they like you, they let you know; otherwise there isn't much you can do."

"Never thought of it that way."

"Obviously, we only put our feelers out to those that catch our fancy, but when asked why I am seeing so-and-so my response is always that when I gave her my number she called. From here on out, as long as she returns my calls we will be dating. What about you, any trouble hooking up out here?"

"No, but I'm not sure how long I will be here so I am not looking for anything steady. This town is not really my style; I only took this job because it was the highest position at a respectable firm that I was offered. Like everybody else in banking and finance, I want to work in New York or at least London."

"With this deal, you might have to stick around for a while, don't you think?"

"I think I'm one small link in a very long chain. All I'm doing is taking luggage from you and giving you a receipt. I am supposed to leave the cash in my office; the rest happens after hours. I am not even in the loop of knowing where the cash comes from or who at my bank is handling the deposits. Knowing you, I can guess where the money is coming from, but this is obviously a lot bigger than your own deal. What do you know?"

"I know we are getting paid well to not know much. Let's ride it out and when it's all over we can compare notes and discuss theories."

"Deal."

I understood that as time went by, I would get a better idea of the grand plan, but frankly I didn't really care. Robert was more curious, but he's patient. Sooner or later we would know what was happening and probably who was involved. The plan seemed to be pretty compartmentalized, and it would be best if it stayed that way. It must have taken a lot of planning to get all these pieces in place.

After lunch we went back to the bank and took my suitcases in through the employee entrance to Robert's office. We opened the cases and counted the bundles. Even in $5000 stacks, 3.5 million dollars takes a while to count. I assumed whoever worked the night shift would run the money through a counter and get an accurate count. Robert issued me a receipt that simply said "700 x 5" and stamped it and put it in an envelope. I wasn't sure what to do with it, but I took it and gave him a list of names and amounts for the deposits.

"Do you know the names on this list?" he said.

"Personalities, most of them; actual names, no."

"Then I certainly don't want to see them. Put it in an envelope and seal it; we'll put it in one of the cases. If we are getting paid to not know, let's do it well."

"Easy so far." I wanted to ask how much Robert was getting paid, but thought better of it. I knew my cousin and Pat were getting paid from the profits of our partnership, but Rose hadn't added any other expenses. I wondered if she forgot to tell me, or if the others had their hands in a different part of the pile.

Agreeing to meet Robert after work, I went to my hotel for a nap. I had partied pretty hard over the weekend while exploring the clubs and felt a little drained. I woke up to a phone call from Robert at 4:30, saying he was going home to change, but he would pick me up around 7:00. I smoked a joint and got sucked into some bad movie. I don't watch a lot of TV and a high percentage of my viewing occurs in hotel rooms. I don't have a TV at home and somehow the central placement in a hotel overcomes my resistance, leaving me helplessly absorbed in whatever schlock is on. At 6:00, I jumped in the shower and dressed for a night on the town. When Robert arrived, he had a six-pack of Sierra Nevada Pale Ale and we smoked some weed and drank the beer before heading out.

He took me to an Italian restaurant that he said was the closest thing we would get to Little Italy this side of the Mississippi. It had been opened by a couple, refugees from New York, and was doing good business. After a big, heavy meal and two bottles of Chianti we were moving a little slowly and I thought we were in for a quiet evening. Robert had other plans.

"Here," he said, holding out his hand. "It's a little speedy so I thought we'd just take a half a hit to give us an energy boost."

"Where are we going from here?" I asked as I put the paper under my tongue.

"Well, you asked me about chicks and I told you I wasn't into dating steady, but I have developed a plan to keep my sex life alive. I don't want to date someone who is looking for a husband, so I date freaks. Freaks self-destruct before relationship sets in."

"You make it sound like an infection, or a cold front."

"To me it is. I am too young and have dreams that run

counter to the concept of being tied down. So, where do you go to meet freaks, sexy freaks that is, who are looking for a good time?"

"I give up."

"Strip clubs. The women are fly and looking to have a good time. Most guys who go to strip clubs are jerks or older and married or both, so I have no problem meeting the dancers. Most of them don't stay in town too long or are so twisted they can't really deal with a relationship so—voila! My own personal dating service. Let's go."

The first rush of the acid hit me as we pulled into the parking lot. It pushed a few yawns ahead of it as it washed over my brain. We smoked a fatty in the car and stepped into the electric vibe of the club in a full body rush. The flashing lights, mirror mosaics, glitzy furnishings, and fog from the smoke machines kicked the dose right into full gear. Robert paid the cover charge and we were escorted to a table. The chairs were low and plush and I felt like I was sinking into a cloud as I sat down. It felt like I sank twenty feet as my perception kept refreshing in tilted frames that became a tunnel out to the environment around me. Only when I settled into a static reality did I notice how beautiful the women were. Weeknights are money-makers at high-end topless clubs, because that's when the expense account crowd patronizes such places. This means that the prettiest women, and the most of them, work during the week. The weekenders are mostly frat boys and lonely guys who couldn't get a date, and the dancers don't make nearly the money that they make from the businessmen.

I realized that this was a very upscale establishment. This thought was supported by the price of the drinks.

Our cocktail waitress, whose name was Brandy, told me the price when I ordered a top-shelf Scotch so I wouldn't be surprised when she brought the drinks. To make sure she realized that she had gotten the wrong impression about us, I paid in advance, giving her a hundred-dollar bill and telling her to keep the change. The smile she gave me assured me we would get excellent service.

Most of the seats were filled with older men in business suits and the dancers were kept busy. It was a good thing their dresses were so easy to get in and out of because it seemed like a film loop of women dressing and undressing. The selection of women lacked the variety of a New York club, but made up for it with a stellar representation of American beauties. Out of thirty or so women there were three ebony women and two Asians and they were in constant demand. A few dancers were having conversations and drinks, but most were in circulation and rarely made it more than ten feet before they had their clothes off again. Because we didn't fit the profile of big spenders, we were lucky to have a good half hour to settle into the atmosphere and our buzz before we were approached. Then one of the girls recognized Robert and came over.

"Hey, sugar," said the brown-haired, green-eyed bombshell as she poured herself into his lap. "Where have you been? I've been trying to call you since I got back into town last week. Is your answering machine broken again? I figured I would have to come over and knock on your door to find you. Who's your friend?"

"Hunter, this is my friend Chris. Chris, meet Hunter."

"You showing off the sights to your friend? I didn't see you in here all last week. Hmmm, couldn't have anything to do with Annabelle going back to L.A., could it? Maybe you can fit me in your date book again now."

As she said this, she gave Robert a wink and told me to enjoy myself as she got up and left us.

"Damn. You hit that?"

"Yeah, and probably will again. She is very cool and loves to party. She is also pretty smart. She is working her way through medical school. Whenever I need a date for a work-related function I call her. Most of these girls wouldn't work for an affair with my co-workers. It is funny too. When the old farts who run the bank recognize her from the club, they have trouble thinking for the rest of the party."

I had noticed a masseuse working the room and when Brandy brought us our third round, I asked her to send her over. A few minutes later an attractive woman with a strong frame came over and introduced herself as April and offered us massages. I told her to do Robert first and as he melted under her care, I took in the sights.

There were three women dancing on the main stage, one on a piano to the right, and two on a stage behind the bar to the left. Walls of mirrors allowed you to see most of the club from any angle. The sound system was excellent and though it wasn't too loud to talk over there was enough bass to feel the music. The DJ, who thankfully didn't feel the need to talk all night, was playing great tunes. As I sipped my drink, I felt my consciousness slide deep into my brain and I let my vision blur ever so slightly. The high-tech light show and the writhing bodies sucked me into a trance in which time and space became fluid and I was hardly aware of my body. I felt like my inner spirit was looking through a tunnel that pierced my construct of self and looked out on an alien world.

From the depths of my trip I was ripped back into my body by the incredible sensation of April dragging her fingernails back and forth across my scalp. Then she massaged my earlobes and face. She rolled my eyebrows between her fingers and kneaded my jaw muscles. Rivers of sensation roared through my brain as goose bumps washed across my body. Just as she settled into my neck and shoulders Robert directed a very attractive woman with large, natural tits to dance for me. As she molded herself between my outstretched legs and rubbed herself all over me, I felt completely seismic. She let her long hair dangle around my head as she pressed her chest into my face. Then she turned around and lay back against me, cupping her breasts with one hand and tickling my ear and neck with the other.

"Happy, baby?"

"Very."

The sensation of getting a lap dance and a massage at the same time was phenomenal. It went on for a few songs before I had to call a timeout. Robert and I argued over who was going to pay as money flowed out of our pockets. We said no to more dances for the moment but were helpless when April told us she also did feet. One at a time she took off our shoes and blew our minds doing reflexology on our feet. I get a lot of massages and can say with some authority that she is really good. Combined with the sensory overload of the environment, we were in heaven.

Who knows how much money we spent. I wasn't sure how much cash I had on me when I went in, but I must have spent a grand and Robert that much again by the end of the night. There were points when we were picking out girls two at a time to dance for each other, and we kept April busy all night.

It was after midnight when Hunter joined us in her street clothes. I was amazed at the difference. With the makeup stripped away and jeans and a pullover shirt replacing the party dress she looked completely different. Still sexy, just different.

"You want to get out of here?" I heard Hunter ask Robert.

"I can't abandon my friend; he's only here for a few nights."

"What if I can find us a fourth? We could go to my place and party some more."

"What do you think, dude?"

"Sounds fine to me."

Too high to drive Robert's car we piled into Hunter's and we were followed by April in her car out to Hunter's house.

"April's one of the few people from work I can hang out

with. The rest are mostly bimbos," said Hunter.

We arrived at the house and Hunter pulled out some wine. My trip was roaring, and thanks to my midday nap I was totally energized. Robert was mellow and sat with his arm around Hunter, who seemed happy with the attention. I could tell he was slipping into a cuddly mood and I knew it wouldn't be long before they disappeared into the bedroom. I, on the other hand, needed to burn off some energy and looked for the stereo and the music collection. I found a dance mix of Prince's "When Doves Cry" and played it. I was in a goofy mood and started silly dancing. I guess it was contagious because when I invited April to join, she readily accepted. We were soon dancing with the abandon of children attempting the silliest moves we could imagine. When Robert and Hunter left the room, I was dancing with a chair and April was putting on a light show, dancing around with a lamp. I did a few somersaults over the back of the couch, while occasionally giving April a "Saturday Night Fever" spin. When the lengthy remix was over, I crumpled to the floor and April fell on the couch, giggling.

"That was so much fun," she said. "I haven't felt so unrestrained in years. It's such a burden being grown up. It feels good to let it loose sometimes." She noticed the contortionist position I had assumed and commented, "That can't be comfortable."

"It's my new stretching technique. I call it 'Silly Stretch.'"

"You are silly."

"Thank you."

"You want to get in the hot tub?"

I untangled myself and popped up with such a look of enthusiasm that she laughed at me.

"Are you always this funny?"

"Close, but tonight I have some acid helping. So where's the hot tub?" I must have looked as excited as a puppy and April laughed harder.

"You laughing at me?"

She managed an affirmative nod through her giggles.

"Well, I usually charge for my service, but for you it's free. Which way to the hot tub?"

"Out here," she said, leading me out back and turning the deck lights on low.

"We don't have suits so we'll have to go naked."

"That doesn't work for me. I'm kind of bashful."

"I'm not convinced. My guess is you are comfortable in just about any situation."

"My cover is blown?"

"Yep."

"Damn, I thought I had you fooled." I said as I began to undress.

"Wait. This might seem weird, but can I do a strip-tease for you."

"Hmmm. Sounds painful."

"You seemed to manage alright at the club."

"Yeah, but they were professionals. I'm afraid you might fall or something and hurt me. Or worse, you might not have that trick of the trade that keeps you from actually turning me on."

"Shut up, you silly thing. I'm serious."

"I don't get it. Mild-mannered masseuse in the den of the lascivious, and now you want to strip?"

"I've never done it before, but I watch it every night at work. I certainly wouldn't want to do it all night long, but dancing for a stranger is exciting to me. You seem pretty cool, and I feel comfortable around you."

"You sure you won't hurt me?"

She gave me a little slap in playful frustration. She went and put on a slow song by Chicago and blushingly came and stood before me. The lights were dim and I tried to be supportive. She did a great job. She had learned a lot watching the girls at the club. Her slight embarrassment and first-time-out blush made it extremely sexy. When the song was over, she darted for the tub, calling out, "Last one in is a rotten egg."

"That was great," I said as I joined her in the hot water. "As I imagined, you don't have the air of a pro and I got turned on."

"I noticed. That made it even more exciting for me. What should we do now?"

As she asked, I dove under the water and attacked her. She was giggling as I pulled her under the water. We came up holding each other and kissed a little bit. Though my body suggested otherwise I was feeling too goofy and high to think about having sex, so we just held each other and kissed some more. We were still in the tub when Robert came out and said he had to get going and had called a cab. I jumped up and said I was ready. April was a little disappointed, but I gave her the name of my hotel and asked her to call me later that day. She knew I was high and let me go, saying she would call.

When we got to the cab. Robert said, "Dude, you didn't have to split."

"I like to let them run a little once I set the hook." I don't fish but the analogy felt right. "She'll call tomorrow and we will see what develops."

April called and we had dinner. I told her that I would be in town every couple of weeks for a couple of nights. I thought it was better if we didn't get anything serious going, but if she was available it would be great to have dinner or go dancing on the town. She said that all sounded good but she fully expected me to come home with her and make love all night. I think she surprised herself with her boldness, and I cheerily accepted.

We spent most of the night getting to know each other, physically and emotionally. She was very sweet and had plans to raise alpaca on a farm she had already bought. Another year or so and she would have enough money to start her own business, though she would probably stick with the job at the club a few nights a week until the alpaca thing took off.

With only a few hours' sleep, I was exhausted when I headed for the coast in the morning. I sleepwalked through the load in Garberville and was with my cousin at the loading dock before I knew it. Pat arrived early Friday evening and he, Carla and I unloaded the truck and crated up the loads to both New York and L.A.

"My shadow was pretty subtle," said Pat. "I couldn't help doing a little maneuver so I could get a look at them. Looked like two young government types, probably military. I took an exit and swung around behind a gas station, making it look like I was making a run for it. In their enthusiasm they drove right past me. I don't think they know I spied on them."

"Probably shouldn't have done that. The last thing we want to do is make somebody nervous."

"Sorry, I couldn't help myself. They probably didn't think anything of it. They picked me back up when I pulled out of the station."

"I'm sure I'll hear about it. Here's your cash. I'll see you in three weeks."

Carla and I spent Saturday bumming around the city and by sunset Sunday I was back on Karen's deck overlooking the ocean.

Chapter Eleven

America was changing. By the time New Year's rolled around we had done two moves out of Northern California and I had given myself a crash course on recent economic history. All the time on planes gave me plenty of time for reading and I couldn't help wondering what the power elite was trying to accomplish with the plan I was deeply involved in. The manufacturing base in America was eroding, giving way to the cheap labor and robotic manufacturing of Pacific Rim states. American service sectors were growing, but there was concern that losing the manufacturing base would threaten U.S. economic power. There were impassioned pleas to reverse this trend by protecting industries with tariffs. Though this flew in the face of the free market ideologies America espoused to its trading partners, steel, automotive, textile, and electronic industries cried for protection. Nowhere were the voices as loud as in the computing industry.

By the mid-1980s American companies that made chips and other computer components were taking a big hit. Investors had become weary of claims about the computer revolution, and the flow of capital slowed down. Further, Asian chips and circuits were making inroads into domestic and international markets. By the mid-'80s, the stocks in companies like IBM and Hewlett Packard were way down and inventory was not moving off the shelves. In 1987, amid rumors that the government would move to protect the industry with tariffs, tech stocks and the market in general raged. From January through September the market showed strength and investor confidence in the computer industry looked strong. Then, on October 19, 1987, the Dow Jones suffered a record loss of 23 percent.

Though the market closed out the year up 2 percent, it had

lost its momentum and investors looked for the safety of the bond markets. Capital expenditures in research and development went down. The excitement in companies promising innovation was low. In part it was the industry's fault. The industry was split with IBM, Wang, and many smaller companies building mainframes and supercomputers that cost $75,000 and up, and on the other hand there were consumer devices that were either glorified typewriters with green screens or home arcade games. The fantasies of integrated, computerized homes and platforms that would be useful for small businesses and individual consumers had deflated. The infrastructure was also slow in bringing innovation to the marketplace. By the time a manufacturing facility was ramped up for production, the technology had become antiquated. If American consumers wanted the latest technology, they often had to look to Japanese imports. It seemed America would lose its place as the leader of the computer industry the way it had the consumer electronics industry.

America needed a business revolution to create a computer revolution and Nathan and his friends seemed to understand this. It was no surprise that they focused their attention on Silicon Valley. Areas outside Boston, Dallas, and Seattle were high-tech zones, but the area around San Jose had more potency. Besides its existing industry, Silicon Valley had two aces up its sleeve: PARC and Stanford University. Xerox's PARC, or Palo Alto Research Center, was the great think tank of the computing age. Though Xerox didn't commercialize all the innovation that occurred at PARC, it was largely recognized as a powerhouse of ideas. The fax machine, the PC, and many other ideas were born there and Xerox allowed these technologies and the engineers who devised them to leave and find new homes. Many ended up as start-up businesses. Stanford University also had the trait of allowing R&D performed under its red clay roofs and the innovators to enter the private sector. The Dean of Physics at Stanford had started his own business selling CAT scanners and laser scanners with ideas he developed during his tenure. Magnetic Resonance Imaging (MRI) was also developed at Stanford and the professor responsible had created his own company, which was located just around the corner in the industrial park where my cousin and I were shipping thousands of pounds of weed. The location of these two think tanks and the freedom for engineers to privately commercialize their ideas made Silicon Valley ripe for Nathan's intentions.

I headed to Santa Cruz during the week between Christmas and New Year's. With the family obligations out of the way and the second load sold, I headed back to my little hide-away in Karen's arms. The plan was for me to head down to L.A. on the 2nd or 3rd to pick up cash from Simon, who was happy to pay in advance, and Nathan would fly out with the cash from New York and meet me in San Francisco. Also, a few more growers had joined our collective and Nathan had to get the names for the new bank accounts. I had my hands full with shipping the weed and selling it and was thankful he was flying out to straighten out the banking reality. We were moving quickly and needed to make sure we didn't make any mistakes, and since I wasn't privy to the big picture, it was up to Nathan or Rose. Nathan said he had a meeting in San Jose, so he would make the trip.

Something about smoking Cali weed in California feels so natural. Perhaps I was feeding into the macrobiotic craze that was the latest vegetarian trip, but consuming a product in the environment it was grown just felt natural. Sitting naked on Karen's deck, I rolled an extra-long joint and smoked it, looking out at the ocean a few miles away. I don't think fat joints taste as good as ones that are cigarette width or thinner, but long joints last longer, and more is more. Karen helped a little, but mostly I smoked alone while strumming a guitar.

We were going to spend a few days at her house, then head up to the Bay Area for the New Year's show.

Karen came out on the deck and took the joint. She stood near the redwood railing with her feet planted squarely apart. The sun caressed her nakedness and tried to fight its way into her thick pubes. With the joint hanging in her mouth, she gave her body a stretch. Her hands came down from over her head and ran up the sides of her torso until they cupped each breast, taking the weight. She looked like an Amazon warrior, with her taut legs, muscular ass, long hair, and a silver band that wrapped around the bicep of the arm closest to me.

"Do you think we should go into town tonight? There is a good reggae band playing at a place near the beach."

"Hard to think so far into the future. Right now I am firmly rooted in the present."

She looked at me and saw me gripping my hardness with a hungry look on my face. She proceeded to take the guitar and plant herself on top of me.

"I think it's my turn to do all the work." She lifted my sunglasses and looked deeply in my eyes as she rocked back and forth.

Being on the receiving end allowed my mind to become uninvolved. I was distracted and let her take pleasure as my mind drifted to the biz. I kept my eyes locked on hers but my thoughts were no longer in the moment. I was trying to sort out what Freedom had said about what might be happening. Rose seemed pretty clear on how the money was to be used, but I don't think she knew the process. Maybe nobody did. Maybe they were just winging it, waiting for a moment to develop. Surely even if we got to fifty or a hundred million dollars a year, it would be small change in the big picture. If the money was targeted specifically it could make a difference, but what was the mechanism? How could Nathan and company feel so confident in their prescience? Were they bluffing? Maybe they didn't care if they lost all the growers' cash. I felt myself becoming more and more curious about what was going on.

When Karen came down from her orgasm she said, “Hello. Anybody home?”

“That was beautiful,” I said, coming back to her. She collapsed on me and I slowly deflated inside her. Most girls needed to have their partner release their energy to feel a sense of completion. But Karen was very self-confident and comfortable with her sexuality. She knew that when I wanted release, I would go for it and she was not bothered by my unpredictability.

We never left her property until New Year’s Eve. We headed north early and partied all day outside the show. She didn’t feel like tripping, which gave me license to go full bore. That year there was some acid going around called the worlds. I had already taken a bunch over the past few months and knew it was clean and mellow. It came in strips five by twenty. There were four prints on each strip. Each five by five square had a row of question marks at the bottom and a picture of the world on a blue background. As soon as we got to town, I ate the five question marks and two hours later I ate the world.

I was thankful to have Karen’s arm to hold onto as the rush came on. We giggled around Grateful Deadland and by the time it came time to go into the show my cheeks hurt from smiling. The show was a fanfare of heavenly delights that seemed to jumble my senses. I heard colors and could see the sound float across my vision like some ancient text. I felt like I was at a banquet with the table full of sensuous morsels. Jerry’s licks caressed my body like a lover’s anxious hands. I danced, sometimes in my own feverish whirl and at other times with Karen as intimately as intercourse. We weren’t alone, it was an orgy that everyone partook in. I was as alive as I had ever been. I was shown all the terrifying brilliance of life while cuddled in the glistening melodies. The lights and sound and colors composed a multi-faceted gem that was infinitely evolving, folding every aspect of humanity into its construct.

During one of the set breaks, Karen asked me if I was okay, as I hadn't spoken for a while.

"Awesome," I said and paused. "But if I had to get gas right now." It was the best formulation I could offer. I was blazing, soaring high on the most courageous tissue of consciousness, but knew that the other world, the place where we spend most of our lives, could present an insurmountable challenge. The bliss of freedom that I rode, like a surfer riding a wave, was incongruous with that other world.

She produced a grapefruit that we shared while sitting in the halls during break. Its texture and flavor were magnificent. I became almost fiendish as we deflowered this gift from the gods, this fruit of ecstasy. Somewhere in my revelry I noticed another presence sitting next to us. I felt a primal urge to protect my treasure. I didn't look up from my sticky fingers until Karen knowingly rolled another grapefruit to me. I looked and saw Robert in full Deadhead regalia. He wore a tie-dye shirt, Guatemalan pants, leather sandals, and some wooden hippie beads. He gave me a smile that extended past his ears and threatened to split his head in half.

"What's up, man?"

"I ate the world."

He looked at Karen, who explained, "Twenty-five hits."

"Radical, dude."

He and Karen talked for a while. It didn't occur to me at the time that they had never met. Somehow the acid and the Grateful Dead made it feel like we all knew each other. Their conversation didn't really register, but I heard something about a party in a hotel room. Most of the talk of that other world couldn't connect to where I was at. As I finished the second grapefruit, the lights went out and the band came back on.

After the show we embarked on a mythical voyage to a land called 'Party.' It seemed that Karen held the key to unravel the mystery to its location and provided me with the needed instructions. After many perilous junctures where magic seemed to facilitate our endeavor we arrived, heroes, at the final part of the journey on a magic carpet ride. When we got off the elevator I was as high as I'd been at the show and showed no signs of coming down. Luckily, I was in a perfect environment for such a state, and nobody thought it too strange when I entered the room and took off my clothes, which had been trashed and a little bloodied during our epic journey. The shower was awesome. Karen pulled me out after a half hour and convinced me to wrap a towel around me.

She parked me in a corner with a pile of buds, which I commenced to roll and distribute. It was the Golden Fleece that I now shared with my loved ones, brought back from the nether world. There was beer and cocaine and tons of weed and people seemed to flow in and out of the room like a river. Apparently, there were other worlds that these people could reach through a space-time portal that opened from Party. I was content to stay where I was and at some time around sunrise Karen convinced me my clothes had been washed and I should put them on. I was fairly out of my mind right up to when I passed out at Karen's.

Karen's was the perfect place to recoup from the trip I had taken. When I woke up, my serotonin was low but I felt reborn. The heavenly lights I had danced with were still lingering at the edge of my perception. The sunshine and Karen's cooking worked wonders and by evening I felt recharged and was firmly back in that other world that had seemed so distant the night before.

Vegetarian food, California sunshine and Karen. It was tactile and as real as can be, but still somehow distant from my life. We made love, sang and danced in the sun and an eternity passed.

Holding each other in the hammock she asked, "What do you want?"

It reminded me my cousin had asked the same thing. I told Carla I had a desire to experience so many things. Not individual experiences, but a collection of experiences that is worthy of calling a life. I just didn't want to get stuck in the wrong one, but meanwhile time passed and my lack of decision led to continuation of my involvement in illegal enterprise. The irony of Karen was not lost on me. If I had answered what I wanted in a life partner, she would fit the bill perfectly. Professional, freaky, healthy, beautiful and easy-going. All that was obvious to me, but I told myself we didn't know each other well enough. Part of it was definitely fear-based. She had gotten her degree and a comfortable life that had the scent of groundedness. I, on the other hand, had dropped out of college. I hadn't planned on it, and still imagined going back to finish a degree, but in what? I wasn't sure if I could slow down and live a life when there were so many options.

"I want to sail to distant ports, eat exotic food, and meet interesting and weird people. And to dance and sing and make love."

She looked at me with patience and understanding and sighed; she knew I wasn't ready.

Leaving wasn't easy. It was yet another world my life was on and in the morning of the 3rd I put Karen in my rearview mirror and headed down to L.A. I stayed with Jeff overnight on his boat. Rene was out of town, but he assured me they were on to something and thanked me again for the introduction. In the morning I met Simon and headed back to San Francisco.

I met Nathan at his posh hotel in the center of the business district. The Hotel Meridian was a couple of years old and as expensive as they come. I wasn't surprised he hadn't chosen one of the more artsy hotels. Though he had dabbled in counterculture, and was entwined in a sub-culture endeavor, he couldn't escape his upbringing. I considered walking in wearing a tie-dye, but thought better of it. I stopped and bought a suit and some shoes to try and blend in. I felt like an imposter as my leather soles waded through the thick carpet of the lobby. No one raised an eyebrow as I headed toward the elevator bank.

Nathan seemed pleased to see me in a suit. I could see a thought flash across his face, as if for the first time he saw a potential in me he hadn't noticed before. I knew he wanted me to see it. Nathan is a consummate negotiator and could be one hell of a gambler because he is firmly the master of every muscle in his face. His perfectly contrived nature doesn't let anything out that hasn't been thoroughly considered.

"I don't think we both have to go to Sacramento," he said. "I'll take the cash up there and you go to Garberville by Friday for the next load. I'll sort out these accounts; we certainly don't want to lose track of money because we're making it too fast. How you feeling about your driver?"

"I think he is working out fine. How do you feel about him?"

"Good, but you never know with Vietnam vets."

Nathan should have been a diplomat. In those few words he let me know that he had checked out Pat thoroughly and that Pat's little maneuver had been noted.

"Hey, how is everybody else getting paid in this thing?"

I knew right away I shouldn't have asked. I knew he preferred me not being curious. He looked at me while he weighed his words. I was in a central position and he knew I would end up with a more complete understanding sooner or later. I think my curiosity worried him as much as it gained his respect.

"You mean like Robert?"

"And the other banker types."

"There is a back end to this deal for the bankers. I'd like

to leave it at that."

He was going to leave it at that, but then thought maybe he needed to say some more. "Listen, this whole thing is pretty complicated. I'm trusting you on Rose's word, and part of that word was that you'd be discreet. I like you and understand you are assuming a lot of risk here, but it will take a while for us to develop the kind of trust I would need to have to share any more than you will find out in the course of you doing your part. It would be best if everybody stayed focused on their part and didn't spend too much time talking."

"Deal. Robert and I already came to that conclusion. But you know, the growers are a little different; they're smart guys and it's their money. I play dumb, but you have quite a reputation among them."

"Well, let them talk. Keep your finger on their pulse and keep me posted; for now tell them that we will be making the first investments this summer."

"Okay, boss."

That got a smile out of him. I couldn't help but fall under the influence of this man. He was a force that was undeniable. He could tell the effect he had on me and was confident I would play it his way. I had a lot more questions, but knew answers were not forthcoming, so I split.

I left his room and screwed a cap on my curiosity. I was thankful to be on the team and knew I was making a ton of money. I wasn't sure how much, but I knew it would be more than I could make on my own. I was young and felt lucky to be making such big moves.

The move out of Garberville went smoothly, as did the next one and the one after that. By the end of March we had exhausted our supply and I was sitting on a half million in cash. I bought my mom a house, and furnished it. I talked my sister into staying in school and paid for it. My teenage sweetheart wanted to move and I helped her with a down payment, moving charges, and home furnishings. I was feeling blessed to be able to be so generous. They talk about marijuana being the gateway drug. It certainly was for me; it was the gateway to the upper class.

I was leaking cash like a broken-down dam. In April a half million looked like a lot of money, but I showed that stack who was boss. By September I was almost broke. My generosity and a bunch of trips abroad had siphoned off the money faster than I had thought possible. Luckily, money was still trickling in from the delivery service, but I told myself next year I would save some money.

Chapter Twelve

Rose outdid herself with the delivery service. We weren't the first to deliver to offices and homes, but we had a cover that couldn't be beat. Other services sent out kids in street clothes who more often than not were wearing obvious signs of drug culture. We bought uniforms. Our messengers weren't clean-cut, but at least well-kempt and carried clipboards and forms and presented themselves in a professional manner. Receptionists and co-workers of our clients never batted an eye when our messengers showed up with a delivery that could only be delivered to the intended recipient. We sold only by the ounce and the packages were sealed so they didn't smell. We put them in padded envelopes with business-like markings. The word spread like wildfire. Bankers, brokers, lawyers and other professionals told their friends about the quality of our product and discreet service and our business grew exponentially.

We ended up selling out in August, but we were lucky to be able to buy two hundred pounds grown in Maine to hold us over. Maine's growing season ends much earlier than California's, and though the product wasn't quite as good, it did the trick. We knew that next summer we would have to hold back three times as much to satisfy our retail operation.

The first year we had deposited 21 million dollars. We were sure '88-'89 would be even bigger. Rose told me that Nathan had confirmed with the growers that the helicopters wouldn't bother them this year. They weren't 100% confident, but they had increased their plantings somewhat. They were also excited by the way we took the product from them up north and they no longer had to transport it themselves. I knew if we pulled it off again the following year would be even bigger as the growers' confidence grew.

I headed out to trim in the beginning of October. I went back to Little Bear's, figuring it would be easier to not talk about the "grand plan" if I wasn't around the growers who were involved.

There is something very meditative about sitting around a table twelve hours a day with the smell of kind bud staining the air. The crew Little Bear had assembled was very cool. There were fourteen of us, including Karen, and a few of the guys had excellent senses of humor. They broke the ice and we were soon all cavorting like old friends. It is funny how quickly we became intimate. We were so open and boundary-free that after the first week we were referring to the hours around the table as therapy.

One of the women was a born-again hippie after years of working as a professional dominatrix. Her stories about her old life were a constant source of hilarity. Any time things got a little dull, someone would request that she introduce another one of her clients. She was mellow, a wholesome-looking earth-muffin type, and I think her stories surprised even her. The level of depravity that some of her clients' sexuality had succumbed to was shocking. Besides her stories she also related tales of her co-workers who performed acts that she wouldn't have dreamed of. Golden showers, defecation and humiliation of all sorts were common themes and never failed to elicit our embarrassment for the human race and its grotesque levels of perversity. When asked how she could have worked in such an industry she replied that she is a pure capitalist. Like trimming, wherever there was profit with only market controls and no regulations, she was in. Somebody pointed out that prostitution and marijuana were illegal; she responded that it didn't matter, they were still driven by pure market forces.

One day I split in the late afternoon, saying I had to meet a friend. Little Bear wasn't psyched, but I was a good worker so he didn't complain too much. Karen knew I had some business in the area that kept me coming out west all the time, but she was cool enough to never ask about it. I guess she figured I would tell her about it when I was ready. I headed down the mountain to look for Charlie Freedom. As I crossed over the river where Rose and I had got it on the year before, I realized she and I hadn't had sex in over six months. I decided I would have to change that, hopefully with one of my girlfriends.

When I got to the restaurant, I didn't see Freedom, but Big Jim was at the bar. He smiled when he saw me and invited me over.

"We usually don't allow migrant workers in here," he joked, "but in your case we will make an exception. Where you working?"

"Up at Little Bear's."

"Don't know him. Shame, I'd like to have you on my crew."

"I hate working for intellectuals; they always get me talking about things I know nothing about," I said, giving him a suggestive glance.

"Good choice. A lot of conspiracy theories floating around."

"I don't know anything, I swear."

"Good kid. What brings you down here anyway?"

"I was hoping to find Professor Charlie."

"He won't be in tonight; we are all meeting later this evening at a friend's for a little birthday bash. Want to tag along? I'm headed up there now."

"Party? Party is my middle name."

"We'll take my ride. Remember, you don't know a thing. I'll introduce you as my nephew so nobody thinks anything of it."

The ride out to the party was mostly on a rutted dirt road that wound up into a canyon. The night was clear and the sky was filled with boisterous stars competing for attention just after sundown. There was no moon and the milky blackness flowed around the points of light. Jim didn't hesitate to show off the suspension of his 4x4 as he bounced up the canyon at fifty miles an hour. I found myself keeping one hand on the ceiling to prevent myself from banging my head on the roof. Jim was oblivious as he tapped on the steering wheel in time to Neil Young's "Harvest Moon." I realized what an apt selection it was for an intellectual who had given up the busy life to live the rhythms of a farmer.

The party was in full gear when we arrived. A few gas lanterns were spread around the yard and about fifty people were milling about. A few musicians were playing off to one side and I heard the twang and screech of banjo and fiddle. A couple of people were dancing and the rest were seated on lawn furniture or standing in groups. There was a keg cooler on a table with glasses and some liquor and another covered with food.

"Let your canines recede a little; you wouldn't want to be recognized as a meat eater. This is a strictly vegetarian party."

"No pig on a spit?"

"Definitely not. Suggesting one would probably land you on a spit."

Jim introduced me to a few people as I put on my party face. The beer on tap was Anchor Steam and I thought how lucky people on the West Coast are to have so many excellent micro-breweries. Once I had a beer in hand, Jim left me alone with a group that was discussing alternative energy. Apparently, one of the guys owned a large store that specializes in renewable resources. The discussion at that point was about inverters to change DC from solar panel and batteries to AC for household use. It was a little technical and I had little to contribute and was feeling self-conscious when Jim rescued me.

"I want to introduce you to our host; his partner is the birthday girl."

"Wife?"

"Yeah, anti-establishment style."

After introductions I fell prey to the proud owner syndrome. It appeared that everybody else had already had a tour of the house and it was my turn. Jeff, whose house it was, insisted that I tour his house, which he treated with the pride of a father whose offspring was ivy-league. It was modest in size but had a large cathedral ceiling in the living room. I tried to act impressed when I realized his pride was in the systems, not the architecture. The house was completely self-contained. Wind and solar power operated 12-volt lights and appliances. Window placement and extensive insulation provided almost all of the heating needs, bolstered by a wood stove on really cold days. The toilet flushed into a composting septic system and the sinks and showers flowed into a cistern that was used for garden irrigation. Of course only eco-friendly soaps were used. I was afraid the tour would include every appliance when we were interrupted by the band singing "Happy Birthday." Jeff bolted downstairs as the last notes were being sung.

A monster truck with more lights than an airport arrived as I bumped into Jim. "That'll be Freedom."

As Freedom made his way through the party, Jim grabbed him.

"You remember my nephew Chris from New York, don't you?"

"Oh yeah. Chris, how you doing?" he said with a conspiratorial grin.

After what seemed like hours of conversations about eco-friendly this, and renewable that, the health benefits of macrobiotic eating, Reagan/Bush bashing, and not nearly enough pot smoking, Freedom grabbed me aside.

"How you doing, kid?"

"I could use some more THC in my blood. I never knew so many straight freaks existed. California is a weird place."

"No doubt. Let's take a walk. This is a strain I picked up in Amsterdam last year. It's called haze. It's not very pretty, but damn if it doesn't grow fourteen feet tall, and it has a powerful punch."

It had a unique taste and the buzz was the heaviest euphoric stone I've encountered. Most weed is either heavy, sort of earthy and down, or psychoactive and light. This was both.

"We gonna have some of this to take home to the folks?"

"Not much this year. I was testing it out. I'll definitely grow more next year. Especially if Nathan says the helicopters won't bother us; fourteen feet is hard to hide. I'll tell you though, not everyone appreciated its qualities. I sort of save it for when I don't mind getting a little stupid." From a heavy smoker like him, that meant it should come with a warning label. "What's new back east?"

"Things are going pretty smooth. I know we ran out of stock for retail and had to buy a few hundred pounds from Maine to hold us over. In terms of Nathan's plan, you probably know more than I. Did you ever invest any money?"

"Yeah. We are all investors in a venture capital group down in Silicon Valley. Nathan said next year we will probably start investing in individual companies."

"Venture capital?"

"You know, the guys who jump in on an obviously good idea after most of the work has been done and by pouring money on it end up owning it. Sort of like a fund that bets all the good horses in a race. The payoffs are high, so any risk and costs are covered by betting a lot of horses. Nathan says that's the way to go for now."

"How do you guys feel about it?"

He knew my allegiance was spread thin and hesitated before he answered. I'm not sure if his answer was the truth or what he wanted Nathan to hear, but it smacked of unadulterated honesty.

"We're in it for the ride. On one hand we are happy to get our cash above board, and on the other hand if we lose it all we can always grow more. By the way, we are going to need some cash this year to offset expenses and to live on. We are creatures of habit and have lived on cash so long we don't know how to use a bank or credit cards."

"How much do you think?"

"Probably the whole first trip."

"What are we looking at this year?"

"Probably 25,000 pounds."

"I'll let them know."

We drifted back to the party. The crowd was a little sedate for me so I went over and joined the musicians. When I got there the banjo was lying down as its owner was playing guitar. I asked if I could play it and lost the next few hours in the music and the haze buzz. The style on the West Coast was different from what I was accustomed to. It drew on many of the same folk and bluegrass songs with some Hot Tuna, Jefferson Airplane, and the Grateful Dead thrown in, but the focus wasn't as much on songs as it was back east; it delved deeper into the jam. I guess it was the Bay Area's psychedelic influence exerting itself, but they didn't hesitate to dig for five or ten minutes into the instrumental textures. All the musicians seemed to be on the same page and I had no trouble blending in.

At three or four in the morning, Jim threw a sleeping bag down next to me and said we were going to crash there. A lot of people had left and I was wondering if Freedom was still there when the smell of Haze drifted through the air. Between songs he came up and handed me a burning joint and a pre-roll he said to put in my pocket. I was thankful because I had forgotten to grab a stash when I left the room full of weed back at Little Bear's. Freedom said he'd look for me on the first Thursday of November and split. At sunrise there were only the musicians and a few stragglers out in the damp air and the light in the sky made them vanish. Left alone, except for a few people bivouacked outside, I turned off the remaining lanterns and crawled off to sleep under the trees.

It must have been around noon when Jim shook me awake and we headed toward town.

"You have a chance to talk to Freedom?"

"Yeah, and he introduced me to Haze. Potent stuff," I said as I lit the other joint he had given me. "He also told me about the investments."

"What do you think?"

"I think I'd be in way over my head saying anything. I can't give you anything concrete, but I can say that Rose and Nathan exude confidence and seem to see all the pieces even if they are not in place yet. I guess I am as curious as you guys to see how it shakes down. You're the one with the degrees. What do you think?"

"Some days I think it is just about the money, and other days I exhaust myself trying to discover Nathan's political motives."

"Well, he is certainly a different beast than the rest of us. His left hand has more corporate establishment genes than the rest of us combined. I don't really get it. There doesn't seem to be enough money in it for him to be taking this risk."

"Which brings us back to political or at least social change. Or there is some way he will make money that we don't see."

"No doubt. What about you, are you getting in?"

"Hmm. I hadn't thought about it. For me it's a cash game."

"How old are you now?"

"Twenty-two."

"If you don't mind, I'll give a little advice. Get an account and play along. It would be a shame if this thing takes off and you miss the boat. It doesn't have to be a lot but get in."

Chapter Thirteen

When the trimming was done and I was waiting to move the first load, I called New York to check my machine and heard a message from Simon. I called him and he said he wanted to meet up and chat. He was taking a trip up north and had been waiting for my call. We agreed to meet in Calistoga in Sonoma County. He was bringing Sebrina and asked if I could get a date. Karen seemed excited and followed me inland in her car.

Calistoga sits on a cauldron of hot mineral water and has numerous hotels that offer natural hot tubs. There are a few resort type hotels that have a full range of spa amenities, but just about every place that supplies lodging has mineral baths and massage. I picked a two-story motel just off the main drag, nestled in a residential community. Even its heating system merely circulated the hot water. Besides hot tubs, this motel also offered mud baths, which was something I had always wanted to try.

Karen and I settled in and then went to meet Simon and Sebrina at a restaurant that had recently received good reviews in *Food and Wine* magazine. Northern California restaurants have an unfair advantage over ones in the rest of the country. The availability of fresh, local produce year-round and the proximity to the vineyards of Napa and Sonoma valleys allow them to put out some great meals. I usually end up eating vegetarian because the produce is so good. All you have to do is wave a bottle of vinegar and squeeze a little lemon over the greens to have an amazing salad. And no matter what you order there is a bottle of wine that will perfectly complement your meal. Even the most modest restaurant that is concerned with quality has a wine cellar that New York establishments would envy.

After dinner we told the women that we needed to talk and suggested they explore the town on their own for an hour. They couldn't have been more different, but they went off with smiles, arm in arm.

"What's this year looking like?"

"More of the same. The first load goes out on Friday; it should be to you by next week."

"How much?"

"Same as last year, I guess, though it looks like we'll have a few more trips this year. What are you thinking?"

"I could do more. A lot more. At least double per trip."

"Things pretty relaxed down there?"

"You know me, I only work with the pros. The feds are cracking down on the Mexican, but all the kind ends up smoked by the more respectable elements. They certainly don't want to jeopardize the lifestyles of the rich and powerful. I don't think we are attracting much attention. You know, I've always been careful, and as always I'll pay up front. In fact, I brought cash with me for the first load, enough for 54 boxes."

He saw I was doing the math.

"1.96 million"

"Well, I guess on the first trip. I'll have to check with my partners about the future. I'll keep you posted."

"I tell you, I'd even be willing to meet you up here to do the deal. I'll bring the cash and truck the weed myself. I feel good about the way the deliveries worked last year, but I'd rather not have the paper trail. I feel most comfortable when I'm the only one who knows where my stash spot is located."

"Well, that sounds pretty enticing. I definitely respect your security concerns. I've had similar thoughts. The more of a disconnect between different parts of the deal the better. Am I shipping the first load to the same address?"

"Yeah, but let's make plans for the second trip now."

"Well, you have the pick-up address from the shipping

records. I should meet you first to get the cash so the money and the weed aren't in the same place. Let's see. Every third Friday, I'll meet you at the Oyster Point Marina restaurant, which is right off the 101 in South San Francisco, at 4 pm Then you can make the pickup at 8."

"You pretty confident about the times?"

"It was clockwork last year. I'm counting on the same."

"Let me give you the suitcases now and I'll meet you in three weeks at the Oyster Point Marina."

I got the luggage and put it in my trunk before we went to find the women. After another round of drinks we split up and Karen and I went back to our rooms. Before we crashed, I made appointments the following day for both massage and mud baths.

We woke to the buttery sunshine cascading through the windows. The outline of the mountains in the distance looked like a fairy tale backdrop with its purple glow. The air was cool, yet held the promise of warmth in its richness.

We had some fruit, cheese, and bread for breakfast and lounged around until our mud bath appointment. I had scheduled the massage right afterwards. The idea was to move right from the relaxing mud bath out to massage tables in the garden. I love getting massages outside in the sun and except for the Caribbean, Calistoga was the only place I knew you could get such service.

The mud bath was bizarre. In the middle of a tiled room was a large, rectangular tub about two-and-a-half feet deep. The attendant came in and told us that we shouldn't step in as the bottom is too hot. The trick is to sit on the edge and move your butt and then your legs onto the top of the mud. Then spread out and wiggle down it and scrape it on top of you. We were also given little foam pillows for our heads.

The mud was a thick, clumpy, red mixture that looked like semi-molten peat moss. It was fibrous and clumpy and fully supported our weight. With giggles that choked back mild revulsion, we settled into position. Spread on top, we slowly shook and wiggled to sink down. I tried to plant my hand to move and found that it really was a lot hotter below the surface. I scooped a handful of the earthy loam and spread it on Karen's stomach and chest. She retaliated and soon all but our heads and necks were under a layer of mud. It was a strange feeling. The heat was very relaxing, but we couldn't help laughing at ourselves for paying to lie covered in a tub of mud.

After fifteen minutes the attendant came in and pointed out the showers and a hose. Extricating ourselves was no easy task. The stuff was like quicksand. As you lifted one part of your body, other parts were sucked down. After five minutes we were finally free of the mud-pit and stood facing each other. Not only were we covered with a fine layer of mud but we had clumps in our pubes. The shower helped some, but the hose really did the trick. We aimed it at each other until we were finally clean of all the mud.

After the massage we retreated back to our room. We made slow, lazy love for the rest of the afternoon. Being around Karen was like a vacation in itself. Our lifestyles were vastly different, and the pace we each attacked life was like the tortoise and the hare. Just being near her made me slow down. Sometimes I wondered how she could be so carefree and indulgent in every moment with no pressure to achieve anything, and at others I wondered how I and my fellow New Yorkers survived the insanity we called our lives. A large part of me wanted to jump off the roller-coaster and settle into her way of life.

"You going to have the same schedule this year?"

"Looks like it. You gonna be around?"

"Well, I've been trying to figure out how to tell you, but I have a man back home now. I told him about you, and he is cool with our relationship, or says he is, but I want to give it a chance."

“He a good guy?”

“I think so. It’s always hard for me to tell in the beginning. I have really enjoyed us spending time together, and I wasn’t looking for someone. He kind of blindsided me. I’m not looking to settle down, but I want to explore this further and doing that and maintaining what we have would make me crazy.”

“It kills me, but I think you should explore it.”

We both knew all that needed to be said had just come out. When we made love again it was with an intensity we hadn’t shared before. We were rougher and more vocal than we had been and all the emotion of our relationship ending worked itself out in the course of the night. In the morning I awoke to her coming out of the shower. I watched her get dressed in front of the mirror. We were both smiling half-sad smiles that were also full of warmth for each other. She kissed me while we stared into each other’s eyes and then she was gone.

I was saturated with melancholy as I drove toward the coast. I had suffered a broken heart in my teens and had protected myself since. I knew I didn’t want to commit to anyone at this point, but watching Karen leave, knowing our relationship had changed, left me feeling something I didn’t expect. We had known that we were voyeurs taking a peek into each other’s lives and had always been careful to not enter into a conversation that would make it something more. What we had was beautiful, and I knew we would always be friends, but couldn’t help feeling maybe I had missed an opportunity, something important that I hadn’t allowed myself to admit.

It was only Wednesday and I had a day to kill. I wished Karen and I had avoided the conversation one more day. It was obvious to us both that once we had crossed that bridge, there was no turning back. Now I was torn between urges. I could go see April or I could go somewhere far away from everyone. April was awesome and we enjoyed each other's company, but Karen had really made me feel something deeper and I realized, to my surprise, that my well-guarded heart was a little broken. I decided to go sit among the redwoods and meditate. The awesome energy of old-growth forests always had a grounding effect and it was there I knew I could best clear my mind.

When I got deep into the park, I headed off the trail until I found a ring of trees that felt right. I took off my shoes and clothes and did some yoga. The thick bed of soft pine needles was spongy and made an accommodating surface. After a good stretch, when my breathing was free and relaxed, I pretzeled into the lotus position and blissed out. I was poked by a few needles as I sank onto the soft earth, and somehow that little bit of pain helped me go deeper into meditation.

I knew I should go deeper, past the bliss to where everything was equal, but I needed the narcotic of euphoria. A shaft of light found its way through the trees and moved across the ring of trees as the sun crossed the sky. When it reached me, I felt a rush of energy shoot through my body. I felt a sensation of vertigo as my consciousness disconnected from my body encased in the sunlight. The wind in the trees played the massive redwoods like strings of a cello, filling the valley with the song of ages past. How relevant was that body sitting in the sun? Its interactions with the cosmos were so minuscule, what effect could it have?

I felt distracted from my disconnected place by the stimulus that was reaching my body. For a moment that seemed to last forever I could both sense the great oneness and the illusion at the same time. My body heard the wind, not the song; it saw individual trees, not the interconnectedness of everything; it felt pain and pleasure, not the intricate dance of life. Why do we have bodies? Why do we exist?

Drifting deeper into this out-of-body experience, I looked

at my body. I saw a fly on my face. It was walking around my nostrils. There was an ant crawling up my leg. The roughness of the pine needles on my skin, the sweet scent in the air, the warmth of the sun, all these things limited my ability to feel the oneness of everything. What was being physical all about? What was the point of all these distractions? Why must we suffer the illusion of separateness? A golden note struck deep in my consciousness and I realized these distractions were the beauty of life. All sensations, good, bad, pleasant, or course were beautiful. Life isn't black and white. We are meant to soar and muck, cry and pray, laugh and scream, and it's all good. The distractions are the beauty of life. For this brief span of a lifetime we were to indulge in life in all its expression. We need to grow down and bask in earthly offerings. Our spirits chose this life, we only need to live it. There is nothing else we must do. Nothing we must accomplish. With this thought I once again felt the seer, the tiny sliver of the oneness that was my ego, take its position back in my body.

"Remain vulnerable to the terrible beauty of life," I thought.

I stood and let the blood flow back into my limbs. I got dressed and headed toward the car. I felt like I was glowing. I hadn't felt so relaxed in a long time. I turned for one last look at the redwoods before climbing into the car, taking a mental snapshot I could recall when submerged in the concrete canyons of Manhattan.

I met Freedom at the restaurant on Thursday night and gave him the cash I had. To make up for the increase in how much I was sending to L.A. I asked him to increase the load to one hundred boxes. I told him I would have the balance for this move in cash on my next trip and would then start making deposits. He was tired and I still felt like being alone, so once business was taken care of, we split and I headed for a hotel.

That started my schedule for the year: ship the weed to New York, sell it, then head back west. I would fly to San Francisco and leave the cash from New York in a safety deposit box and head toward Garberville. Once the truck was on the way I would meet Simon and get his cash. Pat and Carla would crate up the boxes and load up Simon when he arrived. Afterward, I would meet them to make sure everything went smoothly. Then on Saturday I would be at the bank before noon to get the cash from the safety deposit box and head toward Sacramento for a Monday meeting with Robert. I kept seeing April and she was a blessing as I spent a lot of weekends in Sacramento before meeting with Robert late on Monday or Tuesday morning, before heading back to New York. Eventually, April found a boyfriend and gave me the dear-john phone call. To my surprise, all I felt was a desire to call Karen.

I was glad when the last load was shipped. I was spending one week out of three out west, but was on the move most of the time. I felt like a traveling salesman with no roots. Even in New York I was busy and didn't have much time for a social life. I was cautious with women because I didn't feel comfortable revealing my lifestyle, and didn't want to explain my schedule to a girlfriend. I ended up following Robert's model of dating strippers. I was young and had the cash to attract and entertain party girls. I never brought any of them home, always preferring to get a hotel to party in. I was becoming a tourist in my hometown.

Chapter Fourteen

"It's not going to be enough. Fuck."

A weird thing happened in the late '80s: the market for kind bud took off and there wasn't enough supply. What was once sold wholesale in New York City for $3500 a pound went to $5000 per pound and dealers still had trouble getting enough supply. It was great news for the growers, but the rest of us felt the pinch. Luckily, we had set the delivery price at $400 per ounce so we still had a decent margin, but it was a lot less.

Nathan was pacing the floors at the Receiving Department. It was late on a warm Sunday night and the June air was full of optimism. My busy season was over and I knew I had a few months when I wouldn't be jumping on planes. I would have been much more relaxed if Nathan wasn't so tense. I probably should have split, but his energy was so magnetic I quickly became an audience-of-one for his monologue. He was ramping up, posing his own questions while searching for answers.

"The one challenge I foresaw was scalability. We need to generate at least a billion dollars to move this along. Twenty to fifty million, even 100 million per year, is just not going to cut it and I don't see how we can do more biz without taking some incredible risks. I would need 30 receiving departments to get that kind of money flowing. That would require duplicating the entire thing 30 times. Bank, growers, transportation, distribution; it's just not possible.

"Computers are helpful tools but clunky and unattractive to most consumers. Besides gamers, innovation is being driven by business needs. We need to have them in reach of every human on the planet providing personal, social, and commerce solutions. Real-life stuff. I am not even getting to talking refrigerators; I want everyone to have access to information. Malleable, subjective, sloppy and democratic as I agree with Garrett, it is the only way to get to truth. Any one version will be co opted and/or hogtied by its own mandates and will tend to parrot itself in an increasingly myopic cycle of messages that support the political position of the controllers.

"We need to focus more capital. We need to have a bigger voice. We need a marketing arm that will make these investments look sexy, communications that make people feel like they are in the know. As if singled out for this information to the point they lemmingly herd into something that is still a dream. It is like our little group is trying to take a moon shot. We need a bigger team."

It was the first time Nathan had spoken freely to me. We had smoked and had a few fingers of some peaty scotch, leaving him less contrived than I had ever seen him. I can only imagine how it must have looked during some student meeting in the '60s when he ramped up and came to the conclusion that more aggressive, even destructive, methods were needed to get the message of peace out. He was driven, to what end I still don't know. I think he felt himself to be a prankster or heyokha, always hatching grand plans to stir things up. Vishnu-like, he increased the entropy wherever he went, just to annihilate static environments. He carried himself like he knew better than everyone else and, out of concern that there would always be a place for a voice from outside the box, he shook the box. His grandiosity led him to think in societal terms and not just immediate social situations. In fact, he was probably so contrived because he actually couldn't think of himself as part of society and had to put one over on everybody puppet-master-like while he calculated societal forces and grand plans.

"Seems like we have a pretty good medium right here," I said as I lit a joint. "Spreading the word about the delivery service was pretty easy; maybe we can do some sort of whisper campaign."

I was baked and wouldn't have been surprised if Nathan dunced me for my suggestion. Sometimes I should just keep my mouth shut. I see most of life as a series of little problems. Even big problems are just a series of little problems. For me, solutions often come from keeping an idea alive long enough to have a good look at it. Even then it isn't always an "aha" moment, but a slow unwrapping of a thought. Seems something I said connected; without a beat Nathan stole my idea, riffed on it, improved it and put a bow on it.

"Financial capital of the world. Plenty of money here. As self-directed New Yorkers tend to be, there are plenty that aren't painting their own canvases. People want to be in the know. Let's give them something to know. We will start this fall with the Cisco Kid."

War had just done a reunion tour and that was the only Cisco Kid I knew. Before I could even start to dwell, Nathan jumped up and grabbed a container out of his jacket.

"Ever try Ecstasy?" he asked.

"Nope, I hear all the European kids talk about it. I am game."

"Cool, let's go out."

Limelight was mostly over, but if you were gonna go it would be on a Sunday. It was headbanger night and they had a great sound system. Danceteria was gone; my favorite Area was gone. I was happy when Nathan said we were going to The Tunnel. Tunnel was weird, and I like weird.

Growing up in the city it seemed I always had juice. Many of my friends worked in nightclubs and I could get in just about anywhere. It was funny; the first time with a new door person you may have to name drop, but once they got to know you, the line didn't involve you. We walked right up to the ropes and the gates of paradise opened.

As soon as we were inside, Nathan cut out on me, saying

he would find me later. I didn't ask. Tunnel was huge and had many different rooms, themed in different styles. There was a library, an S&M lounge, an almost separate gay bar in the back, and a VIP room downstairs. That didn't include all the other weird spaces decked out with chairs and couches in the crevices of the old train depot. The thing I really liked, something that was disappearing from New York clubs, was the diversity. Clubs were becoming segmented, catering to a particular demographic. That made them boring. Tunnel was one of the few places that still had a mix of clientele. Young kids of all races, middle-aged freaks, drag queens, gays, business people, and a good mix of bridge-and-tunnel may gather in the different rooms throughout the evening, but the dance floor was a cocktail, phantasmagorical in nature, that brought everybody together in one sweaty mass. Did I mention sweat? This was a classic disco where people went to get down and shake their booties. There were wallflowers, and non-dancers standing around, but there was no macho shuffling once you stepped down into the dance floor. If you weren't getting your freak on you were out of place on the floor. Lights, sound, sexy bodies, with everyone custom-mixing their own intake for proper mood coordination. After dancing for an hour it was obvious the Ecstasy wasn't doing it for me so I popped a tab. That did it.

I never got off the floor. I must have looked like a mess a few hours later when Nathan handed me a glass of water. I stopped long enough to drink the water and notice Nathan's dance partner. She was gorgeous, but I wasn't entirely convinced she was a she. To each his own, I thought, and went back to dancing. At 4 am I saw Nathan again and he asked if I was hungry as he and some friends were going to Florent. I needed nutrition after the workout I'd just had and happily squeezed five in a cab to the Meatpacking District. While the other three passengers were perfumed and showing cleavage, I am pretty sure all of us were packing meat.

Florent was a classic, tiled French bistro. Not fussy, but legit. It was always open and the late-night crowd was infamous. It was the late-night rush and there was only a 4-top available and the hostess was not willing to let us squeeze. I saw my downstairs neighbors next to the open table and they had an open seat. I left Nathan with the queens and sat down with some old-school gays. Bob and John were a couple that had moved to Christopher Street in the late '50s and had been at Stonewall and were in Andy Warhol's inner circle. Bob had written a play that was so moving and prescient it inspired a generation of playwrights. They also had the largest collection of Mickey Mouse memorabilia outside of Disneyland, in their apartment. They were great people who always had interesting insight into what was happening.

They were with a woman friend who was straight and they were having a conversation about gay marriage.

The woman espoused the current liberal view that was growing state-by-state: "A couple is a couple. If two people want to share their life, they should have rights of hospital visitation, survivorship, financial cooperation, rights over children, etc. Married couples receive an umbrella of rights that would take numerous documents to come close to covering. That is why I think gay marriage should be legal everywhere. Let's not legislate love."

"They should call it something else," said John.

She continued, "Of course, religious types will have a hissy, but separation of church and state is the law of the land."

"Yeah, but these new gays want to be married in churches," slurred John as I realized he was a little drunk. "They don't get it."

"Churches shouldn't be allowed to determine who gets married and who doesn't. Couples get married in town hall all the time."

"Yeah, but they want to be accepted, which means they want a church wedding and I guess, Daddy walking them down the aisle. Conformists. I am against gay marriage." Drunk or not, John was confusing me. I knew their apartment was in Bob's name and if he died first John wouldn't have the rights to their apartment, or if one of them was hospitalized the other wouldn't have visitation rights, even though they had lived together for 30 years. Longer than most straight couples! Why was John arguing against his own interests?

As if he heard my mind speak, "We are fags, for Christ's sake. We don't want to fit in."

Bob jumped in. "We moved to the West Village from the Midwest to get away from people who wanted to fit in. We were on a vanguard, gay or not, breaking down old norms and crashing through stereotypes. The Beats right through the hippies were all about looking at the world in a different way. Maybe we need another social and legal institution that conveys the same rights but isn't called marriage. And what self-respecting fag would step in a church other than as a tourist, much less seek their blessings in a union clearly not accepted by the religion?"

There was a loud cackling from Nathan's table that caught my attention. It seemed they were comparing penis size under the table, perhaps comparing them to the slab of hangar steak in front of the tallest of the drag queens. Nathan looked at me with a look that said he knows he always brings the biggest gun to the fight.

"Everything about being gay is about being different. I can't understand why they are trying to gain acceptance from the very institutions that have been damning us for millennia. Fuck the churches, fuck the priests. We should start our own religion."

The food was slow in coming, but the conversations kept moving. Bob and John's friend, Linda, turned out to be a lawyer and gave advice to one of the queens who was having a landlord dispute. John and Nathan got into it about soapbox heroes and box top collectibles from cereal boxes during the ’50s and ’60s. Bob, myself and the other two drag queens ended up in a conversation about literature.

One of the “ladies,” whose name was Glenda, offered that she was writing a book on theology.

“What is the topic?” I asked.

“A new school of spiritual understanding.”

“Well, that helps.” I said with a smirk.

“I am motivated by two things, money and spirituality, and thought what would be better than to make money from a book on spirituality? So I invented my own religion.”

“Good plan,” I said in a dismissive tone. Even though I pride myself on being open to truth from wherever it comes I didn’t expect a deep and thought-out tome to be forthcoming from Glenda the drag queen. I ate my shoe once again.

“Were you brought up in a religious practice?” she asked, drilling me with her overly made-up eyes.

“No, but I have faith. Faith in something that can’t be described. Something that is as much an actor as it is a byproduct of human endeavor. I truly feel that the most divine we can be is simply to be a nice person. I don’t need an ethical code beyond contributing to the long and short-term happiness of yourself and those around you. Everything beyond that is unknowable and probably not helpful.”

“Interesting, I agree. I didn’t expect you to have such a clear statement on your perspective of cosmology.”

“The LSD is helping.”

She nodded and said, “Ah. Okay, try this idea out on your psychedelic-addled brain. I call it Abstract Theism and it is the answer to all the troubles of the world, including me being poor.”

She took a breath and started, “The imagery, the scents, the songs, the prayers, all reach to describe the indescribable. Not to say they aren’t valuable; they build an associative network that allows us to glimpse the omniscient simplicity and elegance of the forces that rule what we call our world. In meditation I have seen the light and from the light came streaming the accepted likenesses of gods, saints, Buddha, fantastic deities from the Hindu pantheon, a horse, a lion and many other forms. Setting aside my amazement I rejoiced at the truth and beauty each image represented, but while they were all filled with light, I realized they were actually blocking the light. It was only when I focused my mind on love that the images stopped and what had been a mere backlight moments before grew from a pinhole to a flood of radiant energy that filled my vision and my very essence with the big IT. That force we assume gave a start to this whole thing, and to some extent or another directed the whole universal drama from beginning to end. We recognize it as stronger in certain places or people but still can't quantify or define what it is we feel and if we try to describe the IT that triggered the feeling we would certainly sound like a lunatic. The problem is that the limitation of symbols, words, even thoughts are so constraining as to limit our ability to even conceive beyond what we can describe with words. It is definitely a chicken and egg thing in that no one can say whether it is the language that limits the experience or that our senses limit our experiences to the point of what can be described.

"I grew up Jewish, with those terrible Old Testament prophets who wielded incredible power over the people and even the elements. I swear to Yahweh, they scared the crap out of me. Noah, Samson, not to mention God himself releasing plagues and turning good people into salt. Well, at least one, but that was all it took to scare the crap out of me. I am not sure that that wasn't part of the plan. It certainly kept me inline for a few years as hormones ripped through my teenage mind. Funny thing, these old rules governed my behavior, but I didn't really believe in them. I understood it was allegory, or even exaggerated folk tales written down years and centuries after the events. And it was this disbelief that made me look deeper. For even though I wasn't convinced that any of those people mentioned in the Great Book ever actually existed, there was something about the telling, the hope, the belief in something greater rattling through those ancient tales that convinced me, revealed to me the existence of the light, Om, love, Jesus, nirvana, whatever you want to call it. This needs to be understood in a way that transcends the current limitations of our imagination. We need to have a framework to discuss experiences that can't be weighed or timed or dissected. Only when we start to work with a framework of vocabulary and understanding will we be able to experience more of IT and with more experience the more complex our framework can become which will further inform our experience.

"The beauty of Abstract Theism is that one mustn't change their practice or speak against their traditions to believe. Abstract Theism is merely an expression of the light that illuminates the images we have come to accept, whatever background you may come from."

"So, how do we get there if we can't use words to describe IT beyond whatever imagery we have been spoon-fed from the inception of our life journey?" I asked.

"That is what the book will answer, as well as providing some much-needed vocabulary to carry the conversation to the next level"

"I was really hoping for an epiphany right here in Florent."

"Sorry, honey, you will have to buy the book."

As we finished, the sun was coming up and we had effectively become an 8-top. Seeing the confusion in the waitress's face I walked over and paid for everybody. I walked the few blocks home with Bob and John and fell fast asleep as soon as I was horizontal.

Chapter Fifteen

It was the fall of 1990 and it was working, happening anyway. Selling Cisco Kid and seeing the explosive IPO in the newspaper brought it home. Nathan had run with my idea and used our distribution channel as a promotional campaign, spreading insider information. I can't really say how much of a role it played, but the timing was curious.

It was the first day of trimming and I was once again in therapy at Little Bear's. I had skipped a year and had missed it. Therapy, and the slowing down of time that occurs at the table, has been a source of strength for me, something regular in my life that only came once a year.

I also wanted to see Karen. Though I was unwilling to commit myself, it pained me to know she was out of grasp. As expected, she was there.

Smoking the year's harvest a few yards from where it was grown is nothing short of sublime. I don't think it is the same for connoisseurs of other plants. Sure, there are garlic festivals and corn queens, sap moons and harvest dances for potatoes and beans and squash. Grapes have certainly evoked ceremonies and debauchery throughout history, but all those exertions revel in the mundane. Marijuana connects the mundane with the cosmic.

In the great outdoors, plants grow ten to fifteen feet tall as they reach towards the sun's golden rays. Once harvested, the plants are cut in half before being hung up to dry. After a few days of drying, they are ready to be trimmed. It takes eight to ten hours of trimming to prepare a pound for retail sale. The last of the drying, or curing, occurs while the buds are being manicured. Once trimmed and sufficiently dried, it is vacuum-packed in single-pound, clear plastic bags.

The bags are all labeled with the name of the strain. I

never cared too much about names of weed, as I like variety, and I haven't smoked any variety yet that didn't have its time and place. Names like Bubble Gum, Hindu Kush, and White Widow all describe the general attributes one could expect from the high and there are people at the table who can identify by smell or taste what the strain is. These are hardcore aficionados.

"Dude," said the dude next to me at the trimming table as he passed me the joint. He spoke without releasing much of the air in his lungs, in an effort to hold the pot smoke as long as possible.

With an exhale he said, "What an amazing plant."

He was speaking to the choir and we knew the drill, but were also all guilty of rehashing the same political diatribe on occasion. I think it helped counterbalance the outlaw aspect of being a proponent of marijuana. There is nothing so motivating to a cause as the belief that one is on the right side of the issue. We shall overcome and all that. My father would later tell me that, yes, I was on the right side, but it could have been for a better cause.

"...It grows in every environment, while actually replenishing the soil of nutrients like nitrogen. Its industrial and commercial uses include providing protein, fabric, light oils for lubrication and combustion. No processing or aging, except for some time to dry, or ingredients to add. It is the miracle plant that could save humanity. If it weren't for Dow Chemical back in the '30s..."

It was all familiar. I heard the facts in my head in my own voice. I had bogarted the joint for so long that I decided to roll another. In high school we used to roll joints a few papers long so it would make it around the circle. If I could do that in my lap outside with a wind, I could roll a doozy on the table. It got to be five papers long before I had to call it quits. It lit fine, but by the time it was around the table a few times and was half gone it had become a resin bomb. It was excessive, but when you are surrounded by pounds and pounds it is challenging to come up with new ways to smoke it.

"...Between the plastic companies and the pharmaceuticals lobbying the government and creating propaganda to scare people, no wonder it is thought of as a weapon of Satan."

As he carried on, Karen got up to take a break. I followed her outside.

"Wasn't sure if I would see you this year," she said.

"I wasn't sure I would see you either."

"I am glad you are here," she said as she reached out and touched my arm. Just one touch and I was gone. She saw it in my eyes. She looked apologetic but also available. "I support myself for most of the year on what I make in these few weeks; you knew I would be here. You are the one who keeps a girl guessing."

"Who knows. Maybe you will use that law degree one day."

"Not as long as I can live a simple life. I don't even want to think about the awful wardrobe I would have to wear," she said with a smile.

She had style. Not one you could place, but she had the knack of taking this and that and putting it together in a way that looked elegant yet a bit rough. Not shabby or chic, just cool.

"I was hoping to see you, no expectations, but I must admit a fair amount of desire. How is it going with the new man?"

"Not going. He was really interested in an open relationship, which sounded good until I realized that is not what I really want. I want a witness, not a sex buddy. Being polyamorous sounds good on paper, but to be honest I haven't seen any examples of it really working for all parties. Someone always gets hurt. In our case, it was a string of other women who quickly realized they wanted him for themselves, only to come to grips with the impracticality of that desire. I was fine with the other women, but not fine with the time and heart space he spent trying to put a Band-aid on a wound that won't heal. Call me old-fashioned, but I didn't see it working so I broke it off."

"Well I make myself available to assist in the healing of a broken heart," I said with a playful air. "I am really glad you are here. I didn't come out last year because the thought of you across the table yet so far away would have been too much."

She leaned into me, which communicated more than words. I was filled with peace and joy that was so blissful it was scary. As I put my arms around her, I wondered what the hell I was afraid of.

I rambled, "Trimming for me really has become therapy at this point. I need it. The taunting we give each other at the table leads to self-reflection and quantum leaps in self-understanding. Amazing, none of us have any training, but somehow mass law leads to effective therapy. The group always manages to strip away the bullshit and reflect back the truth of oneself, which is so easily avoided. A chance to take a good look in the mirror."

"What do you see in the mirror?"

"I see love. Not Disney style, though that is part of it. But real blood and guts love. I don't know if that creates a legacy or monument, but to me it would be a hell of an accomplishment if I can tame my primal instincts and act and react with love."

She looked at me with those beautiful deep eyes. You can't bullshit Karen; she is too real. After a pause I started over. "Okay, that isn't it. That is how it looks with bunting and band and posters with slogans. From the base level of politics animus, I see the flaws of humanity personified in myself and love is the method I have chosen to counteract my flaws. Instead of numbering and naming my flaws and fighting them one at a time, love conquers all. The mirror is almost like a scorecard in some karmic game of love versus chaos."

"Hmmm, love versus chaos. Interesting choice of polarity. Not black and white, or creation destruction. Love can be a pole, but chaos by its nature does not hold any ground or have a tendency to be opposed or opposable. Maybe the good and evil/ creation and destruction mythos is too binary. Maybe the cosmos is not about being in one state or another; it is about being in a state or not, with love being the only state of existence and the human, even the universal, saga is about moving towards this state. Maybe that is what black holes are."

She was a black hole for me. She would never ask, but if I were to choose a life with her, she would have me, I am sure. And I have no doubt I would never have cared about what I might be missing.

We kissed tenderly and held each other before going back to work.

Funny stuff comes out around the trimming table; we don't call it therapy for nothing. One beautiful afternoon, the conversation turned to sex. There were five women and six guys. Not women and men, women and dudes.

The women were all on paths of self and social redefinition that looked to find more harmonious ways of living. Casting aside roles and customs and fighting a bias that was all the more clear in their eyes, they became warriors. Peaceful warriors, but with intellect and heart honed for engagement. They had higher barriers to jump and when they jumped, they flew. Four out of five owned property and had some entrepreneurial angle they were working—women whom I came to wish ran the world.

The XY chromosome was represented by sparkling spirits who were well into crafting beautiful life stories, but one couldn't have the same confidence in the stories coming to a happy ending. The life I was living certainly put me in that category as I was constantly reminded by billboards and advertisements about the war on drugs.

There were more than a few giggles as we wound our way through the challenges of engaging in mixed-gender discourse about sex. Two of the women at the table were a couple and came up from San Francisco every year.

"We like toys," said Sasha, the one with the most piercings.

At least three of the guys simultaneously chimed something like, "You should try the real thing."

"Perhaps you misunderstand; we like toys that focus on the outside. Penetration isn't our thing. Penetration is about penises and penises come with men."

Austin, who we all knew was gay, came out of the closet. There was a lull in conversation and he just blurted out, "I am gay. I have always been gay," looking us each in the eye he punctuated it, "I am gay".

"Well, no freaking kidding."

"Who cares?"

"Do you mean you actually thought people didn't know?"

"Austin, you are the epitome of gay. It was totally obvious the first time I met you," said Sasha and everyone agreed. "No secret there."

Austin looked embarrassed, not of being gay, but as he realized his closet door had always been open, he was struck dumb. Still he was relieved with the surprising and light-hearted response his confession evoked.

The conversation turned back to Sasha and Monica. "So what is your problem with men?"

"You are all pigs," responded Monica with a fierceness that revealed a side of her we hadn't seen. "All you do is think with your dicks, no understanding of subtlety or timing. You all think you can have anything you want and have hardly evolved from cavemen, or lizards even." Stopping to light the joint in her hand and compose her thoughts, she continued, "My first fuck didn't last 10 minutes. Absolutely zero communication or connection. It was embarrassing to see each other afterward, even though we were both okay with what happened. I felt social pressure to lose my virginity and he seemed innocuous enough. The expectations were set low and met. He is probably gay too because his first experience was as passionless, loveless, grooveless and straight up lame as mine".

"Innocuous and lame sounds pretty good."

Funny, those moments in life when things get really quiet. Not just in the room or the house or the neighborhood, but almost as if the galaxy held its breath for a moment. So much can be shared in so few words. Beth, whose parents had named her Rainbow and was actually local, was probably the quietest person in the group. Her reticence lent no air to the importance of her contributions, either positively or negatively, though we did make a little room in the onslaught of banter whenever she did speak. Conversation for her went at a slower pace in an attempt to keep things orderly, regardless of what was going on around her. It was obvious this was not due to any lack of intellect; its cause was stern discipline resulting from trauma and chaos.

The awkward silence prompted me, "I was not a willing party to the loss of my virginity." All eyes on me. I moved from a small town to New York City as I hit puberty. I was offered a blowjob in the stairwell my first week of school and was made fun of for a year for turning it down. City chicks were years ahead of the catch-and-kiss I had moved away from. I had to ditch a girl in a nightclub because at 15 years old, knowing she had her diaphragm with her was more pressure than I could handle. I was ready and wanting, but terrified. When I shared the story, I always turned it to an awkward joke saying, 'I would probably still be a virgin today.'"

Beth looked relieved to have the pressure off. I could see

the curiosity in everyone's eyes. Around the table there is never a rush for details. We all know that whomever shares will take their time to tell the story, knowing that hours of question and answer could follow. Everyone waited to see if I would share more or if some other bombshell would drop.

"I was raped." I paused for dramatic effect and to reconsider talking about this at therapy, where we are all like little Sherlocks trying to get every detail and nuance of each other's personalities with no hesitation to offer suggestions or punch lines. Karen knew.

"A bunch of us went out for the weekend to a girl's house in the Hamptons with the promise there would be a lot of alcohol. It turned out to be a beachfront mansion with a pool and the girl had paid the maids to not tell her parents and to help her keep the house in order. She had already slept with a number of the older guys in the circle, including a few that were invited. And though she was sexy and very cool, she didn't line up with the Utopian vision of being swept away I had cultivated and was not the person I would have chosen for such a momentous act. Anyway, morning wood ended when I came as I woke up. She laughed at me for being so quick which added to the confusion I felt while locked in the bathroom for an hour."

"Dude, how is that possible?"

"I hadn't thought about it for years when I read an article in some psych mag about men being raped. It is physically possible."

That started the conversation about initial introductions to sex. The women shared their miserable firsts, two out of five clearly involuntary. The dudes mostly tried to brag, but few held up to the scrutiny of therapy when it came to the level of consent or interest in their counterpart.

"That is what I am saying, they are all pigs," said Sasha, "Even the ones who don't go around humping everything they can like wild dogs, would if they thought they could get away with it."

"Well, apparently some women are equally predatory."

"Maybe, but when you compare the numbers it is pretty obvious that men vastly outnumber women in their comfort using brute force, social power, drugs or any means to get off."

The whole time Karen and I were connected under the table. Our feet touching, or hers in my lap, we slowly worked our way into bliss that revealed itself as we tore each other's clothes off. Our time together had taught us each other's needs; the time apart had made us hungrier for each other. Once we finished dinner and could get away from the group, we were on top of each other. She bit my ear, I slapped her ass, buttons flew, but once we were undressed, we slowed down, way down. A quickie wasn't going to cut it for this reunion.

Chapter Sixteen

Arriving back in New York City after a few weeks in California is always a bit of a bumpy ride. I love both the relaxed vibe of Cali and the intensity of New York, but it can take a day or so to shift gears. I woke up and turned on the computer in case any new messages had come in.

----encrypted message (computer language lorem ipsum)

Staring at my green screen I saw only unintelligible gibberish. Inserting the disk Garrett had given me, the encryption started and after a few minutes I saw a short message of time and place from Garrett.

I was never an early riser and was further conditioned by living the nightlife, making 9 am an ungodly time of day for me. I wasn't alone; the West Village was filled with subculture types and freaks. There weren't too many people with normal jobs. The post office didn't open until 9 and the pharmacies not until 11. The subway station at Christopher Street was quiet during rush hour. My neighbors just didn't get up early. I don't think anyone in my whole building woke up before noon. I could make as much noise as I wanted at 2 in the morning (think bluegrass banjo with the windows to the courtyard open), but if I made noise at 9 it was likely to get commented on by my neighbors.

The next morning I fought off sleep and made my way through the empty streets. The only people I encountered were a few stragglers breaking dawn in their quest for bliss and the girls walking home in their party clothes after crashing at their boyfriends'.

There was a wind off the Hudson and the fall air was invigorating, carrying a sweet ocean tone. In my half sleep I felt a pull to the mythology of traveling the sea. For centuries New York had always been a seafaring town, its commerce and cultural gravity stretching the world over. In another time I could have been walking to the active piers and boarding a ship to some exotic port. Even the lowliest of sailors was guaranteed adventure and tales to tell when he came home. The tropics, China, Australia. Months on the open sea. I was allowing myself to be seduced until a grumbling in my stomach made me think of food. The food on a ship, even for the captain, can't be very good. I don't think I could go without vegetables for that long. Besides, the ride I was on held plenty of adventure. Ain't no place I'd rather be.

"You sure you weren't followed?" asked Garrett as he surveyed the street behind me. Only after being confident I wasn't followed did he let me in the door. It was a brick building in the West Village that was once a furniture factory. There were no markings on the outside of the building and only one large door. Entering the door one walked down a long corridor before the main space opened up on the left. There were tables everywhere and on every table were computers with big glowing green screens with what looked like alien babble in blockish letters. A few screens were actually showing color and there was a crowd around those.

The tenants of this high-tech bunker were an ambrosia of humanity. The only consistent demo/psychographic was age. They were young. Clean-cut and well-groomed or unkempt and shaggy, straight or curly, all members of Garrett's team had a look on their faces that expressed the sophomoric enthusiasm that pervaded the group. Acolytes and devotees of this new paradigm, they riffed with each other and made wild assumptions about how the future would unfold and from whence the threats would come and how to best address them.

Garrett had invited me to meet without telling me why. I had given him a half million dollars and figured it wouldn't stop there. I was curious to see what he was doing with the money.

I didn't expect to see Nathan at the meeting. I had gotten

the impression that the counter-insurgence would exclude the leaders of the insurgence, but Nathan plays a complicated game. It reminded me of Professor Freedom's dissertation on thesis times antithesis equals synthesis.

"You in on this, I asked?"

"Definitely." he said, although he didn't look hopeful when assessing the ragtag team Garrett had brought together. You could tell he was mired in calculations, trying to determine the effect of this cause or that cause played against each other, as if it was some glass bead game.

Garrett stood in the middle of the room and started speaking.

"We are going to witness the greatest advance in human social evolution happen in the shortest amount of time. Society's evolution from hunter-gatherer to agrarian took hundreds of thousands of years. The time between Leonardo's drawings and an actual helicopter was hundreds of years. The scientific revolution and subsequent industrial revolution took centuries, but we are going to see change in decades. What now seems inaccessible and without benefit will be the center of businesses, households and personal lives within years.

"No one knows how it will play out and I want all voices to be strong in the conversation that defines this next stage of social evolution. Otherwise it will be sorted out by corporations and state actors and I can pretty confidently say they will develop a system that won't work in the individual's favor."

Garrett got everybody's attention around the latest computer with Windows 3.1 installed. Built around the latest in chip technology, it was the closest thing to Ada's vision yet. Besides Microsoft's own software there weren't many programs available for the new platform, but other companies were rushing to provide solutions that would work in the Windows environment. He ran through some of the functionality by typing a document in Word and showing off how we could actually see the formatting changes. Then he drew a picture with the 16-color paint program. Then he dialed up Gopher and downloaded some documents from the University of Minnesota's bulletin board.

He kept it moving, but to be honest, it wasn't that exciting. He showed us an online game based on Dungeons & Dragons named Neverwinter Nights, and the emerging world of AOL, where supposedly you could get laid. All of it was accompanied by a cacophony of beeps and screeches from a box connected to a phone line. When he finished, he looked like a kid in a candy store, but was facing a bunch of faces that basically said, "So what?"

"Okay, I get it. The man on horseback probably thought the same thing when seeing his first car. We have a way to go yet before we achieve a useful tool outside of specific settings. But this is where the fight starts. Every one of these programs is written by a company that wants more of your money. To get more of your money they want to know you better. It stands to reason that they will build a means to gather information into the software. And even if they don't, outside elements will seek to exploit the programs and the exchange medium in order to find out more about you. And, we can only hope that the motives will be as benign as making a profit.

"The challenge of this unnamed computer crew we make up is to frustrate and weaken their efforts. We will discover systems that seek to collect data that is unrevealed to the user. We will find exploits before they can have effect. We will push the vanguard of encryption and create an intelligence base available to everyone. And, if necessary, we will attack bad actors directly. The internet must remain without a governing body, except the users themselves, and remain free from subversion by commercial or political entities."

An ideas man who didn't like public speaking, it was easy

to see Garrett's discomfort addressing the crowd. But, through his discomfort and run-on sentences flowed the unmistakable drive of a man on a mission. He was railing against something that hasn't happened yet that would come in forms no one could accurately predict. His goal was to be at the forefront of understanding the implications of this new technology and its social applications so he could see the effects, and potential effects, on individuals and society as a whole.

"Our main efforts will be technological in nature, but we also need writers, philosophers and users to help our understanding of the evolution of this technology and how it is altering the dissemination of information and the flow of ideas in social and business settings."

Garrett was a purist in his desires of how the network of networks that had recently been christened the World Wide Web should evolve. He understood that commercial interests would seek to utilize and control this new technology, not to mention the state actors who would seek to make it a propaganda platform. He wanted it to remain pure information, the best research tool ever imagined by builders of libraries and research institutions throughout history, and available and accessible to everyone. The information would come from users themselves and fact-checking and verification would also be on the shoulders of the users. He didn't want to be sold anything on the Web, as there were plenty of options for commercial transactions. And if there was to be product information, he wanted to be able to find unbiased information about what to buy since he understood that once the information was coming from sellers it would be corrupted.

He finished his monologue: "Thank you very much. Now back to work, most of you. Find out what Microsoft is hiding under the hood of Windows. They have the most to gain, they must be guilty." And, he added, "Just kidding", though it was hard to tell if he was kidding.

Most of the people rushed off to stare into computer terminals and the few standing were ushered into Garrett's "office," which looked more like a nursery school classroom. There were kaleidoscopes, a Newton's Cradle, squishy things to toss, brain puzzles of all sorts and notepads and pencils strewn about the room that still maintained some sense of order. Seating was mostly in bean bags, which made for a funny scene as Nathan navigated his well-heeled coolness into a bean bag. Garrett flopped into a bean bag with an exhaust of his lungs that sounded like it could be his last.

"I am not going to tell you exactly where the money is going if that is what you are hoping for. Compartmentalization, right? The details aren't important, but I will work hard to get the best bang for the buck considering I don't know how long the fight will be and what twists the battleground will take. That, my friends, takes time and money."

Speaking to a smaller group was easier for him. He spoke with fervor, without the volume pushed by nervousness, but still with a firmness born of unshakable certainty. Like a soapbox pamphleteer championing democracy on the corner of Paris or Boston as kings cannoned their way through history with attempts to resist change. A modern Thomas Paine, he would rabble-rouse and shout and carry his message as far as his life would take him.

Leaving the bunker, I had a feeling of elation, like hearing pipe organs in a church, but I couldn't grasp any solid ideas about what I had just experienced. I was an investor in Garrett, although I couldn't really get my head around his efforts to spend my money. He was like an evangelical preacher and had me opening my wallet for the hope of a better tomorrow. I wasn't the only one, Rose and Nathan were throwing money at him as well.

Walking down 7th Avenue, the first hint of fall was in the

air. Harvest time was starting out west and we were starting the cycle again.

"Why do you bother with the trimming thing?" asked Nathan, who had left Garrett's bunker with me. "I would go nuts sitting around a table for days on end. You don't need the money."

I didn't have an answer that would make sense to Nathan, but I tried anyway. "It is like meditation for me; it slows me down to where I am only focused on what is in front of me." I saw a quizzical look cross his face as he wondered why someone would waste time thinking about only one thing. "And the group dynamic is awesome; no matter who is there you become a cohesive group over time. Everybody is in everybody's business but without a personal agenda. I find it healthy."

"Sounds creepy to me. The last thing I would want is a bunch of people telling me what my problems are."

He got quiet and my head was buzzing as I tried to understand Garrett's motivation. We walked in silence for a bit.

"Garrett's wrong, you know."

I looked at Nathan. He shared Garrett's vision of pure information, but knew it wouldn't come to pass.

"How so?" I asked.

"It won't happen without commerce. There just won't be enough force driving innovation if it is just a library you can access from anywhere. Once people figure out how to make money on the Web, the technology will really take off. I am not saying that is what I want, but I am more of a realist than Garrett.

"When radios were first available to the public, the manufacturers of radio also made radio shows so people would have something to listen to. Without content, no one would have bought a radio. Same thing with TV. Somewhere along the way a commercial model developed, first with sponsors, then with advertising in 30- or 60-second spots that pushed the advancement of the technology."

It was still early for me and my brain was having a little fun of its own. I lost track of what Nathan was saying and started thinking of myself as an alien. Over the next few blocks I nodded and encouraged, but was in my own little thought bubble. Walking down the avenue I looked into the faces of the earthlings, living their lives without knowing of the underground weed business or the grand plan to digitize human life experience. Nathan appeared as some wise leader of an expeditionary force leading a small band of us to infiltrate and direct human endeavor while acting normal. Normal was alien to me. I could sense the lack of normal in my life but I didn't know what it felt like or how it tasted, as if I couldn't eat human food.

"We need Garrett's voice, but I am a little concerned with the attention his crew might attract after the feds arrested all those hackers last spring."

"I hadn't heard," I managed to say as I pulled myself out of the walking dream.

"No? It was a big deal. Operation Sundevil, run by the Secret Service. They made raids in more than a dozen cities aimed at the most notorious hackers. There were only a couple of arrests, but it scared a lot of people underground. They were mostly hacking credit card and telephone company networks, but from a technological perspective it is very similar to some of the methods Garrett is gearing up for. I know he was canvassing some of the old-school hackers to get them involved, but it looks like he will have to build his team with newbies."

Standing on the corner of 7th Avenue and Charles Street, the Trade Center framed the West Village and reflected the sun and the beautiful colors in the sky. A few leaves flitted through the air and a warm autumn breeze was blowing. I had nowhere to be until later in the day. Nathan had a meeting and left me on the corner to contemplate the download he had just shared.

I headed down to The Bagel for breakfast. The place was tiny, maybe a dozen seats, and had been a fixture of West Village life since the days of free love, Bob Dylan and Joan Baez. Well-worn and well-scrubbed, they presented the usual breakfast offerings a little better than a diner at twice the price. I walked in and saw a few friends from school. I hadn't seen them in years and wasn't sure about joining or avoiding them. There being no place to hide and no options for a subtle retreat, I joined them.

David, Neal and Peter were what might have been described as nerds in junior high. A bit uncoordinated, super smart, into Dungeons & Dragons, it turns out they had all gone on to do some crazy shit. Neal was a well-known, and apparently well-paid, porn critic. Peter had written a book on his experience living on a park bench and turning tricks in the Meat Market, dressed in drag. David was a lawyer working for a publishing house. They were super sharp and really funny. My guess is they had only stopped doing lines before they came down long enough for breakfast.

"Do you want some candy, little boy?" Neal was recounting the story of Joe, who was an older guy who hung out in Abingdon Square Park, trying to get young kids to come up to his apartment that had a great view of the park, and candy.

He could do an excellent job mimicking Joe.

"Come upstairs and I will give you some candy."

He seemed to get a thrill out of repeating that phrase.

We all laughed at how uncomfortable and weird it had made us feel, except Neal. It was probably cocaine, or maybe he was so out there he talked about it openly. Still, he surprised us with his candor.

"Hell, yeah. I went and got the candy. And he did have a nice view of the park."

"What the fuck, dude? You went up with the old creep?"

"Yep, me and Brian. He had some good candy and he wasn't that creepy."

"What else happened?"

"Not enough for me," said Neal. "I was hopped up on hormones and hoping for some kinky shit. Seemed like the dude was trying to develop a relationship. I just wanted him to touch me."

"You are sick."

"No surprise there."

"I can't believe you would have let him touch you; so fucking creepy."

"People are fucking weird," said Neal. "There was this old guy who I think was the cleaner for a doctor on 30th Street who would pay kids to get examinations after hours. Nothing ever but turn and cough and a finger up the butt. I heard about it from a Puerto Rican kid at school who introduced me to the doctor. I think he got paid for the introduction."

"What the fuck, dude, that is ridiculous. What would he do?"

"He had on a doctor's coat and a stethoscope. I would strip, he would pretend to be a doctor and it was quite normal until he shoved his gloved and lubed finger up my butt for a few minutes. All his attention was anally focused. Never anything more. Then I would get dressed and he would give me fifty or sixty bucks. I went once a week."

"You are a fucking freak," I said.

"Certainly used to be. I have calmed down a lot. Getting laid helped. I have been with the same woman for a few years, and yeah, I feel pretty lucky that I survived the onset of puberty somewhat sane and std free."

"What does your lady think of your occupation?"

"She thinks it is weird and she likes weird. It makes for a good conversation starter at a party. She isn't interested in watching it, but sometimes we have a laugh as I try to come up with a review of the same old shit. Believe me, it isn't exciting at all. Just a living."

Peter was basically nuts. He lived with his mom and it was a mystery to us all that he had focused long enough to write a book as his cognitive flow was frenetic, spirally and thoroughly annotated. He was an entertaining, if sometimes disruptive, contributor to conversation as his inferences were broad and his communication skills superbly acute. But his cognitive processes were like firefly dances or anti-matter; blazing ideas with gravitas and pomp appeared randomly through the conversation topology with narrow sinews connecting them to general flow. His non-sequiturs were nonetheless entertaining and always held some gospel truth. He also had a very unique non-verbal accompaniment to his speaking, very busy fingers. Not just hand gesticulation, but flexing and straining of his digits, as if he was trying to mold clay to fit his meaning. The occasional quick motion was sometimes accompanied by a finger snap and he often invaded the personal space of his audience, but in his eyes there was never a hint of aggression, just an insistent pleading for understanding.

We were halfway through breakfast when David asked me what I was up to. I loved these guys. These beautiful freaks, homegrown, local. Brought up on the same stoops and paved baseball fields, they were my peeps, my homeboys. I didn't want to lie to them, but I was committed to secrecy. If there was any group I would have laid it out for, it would have been these three, but a public place was certainly not the right venue.

Luckily, I was saved by an outburst from Peter, who was reading the *New York Times*.

"Fuck, as if we didn't know they were dirty."

"Who?"

"All of them. Reagan, Bush, the Israelis, Kissinger and all the players at the grand chessboard. They want us to think it was as simple as arms for hostages because they don't think we can understand that we would team up with Israel to sell arms to Iran after the fall of the Shah because we were more afraid of Iraq. Politics as usual is easier to understand than geopolitics and foreign policy. Now we are at war with Iraq and all those responsible for the arms for hostages conspiracy are sure to get pardoned by Bush. Bush's hands are probably bloodier than anyone else's. Are we naive thinking it is a nice world out there and Bush is the bad guy?"

Like a loop-de-loop roller coaster. Provocative, but always a bit cryptic and always leaving you to come to your own conclusion. He disappeared back into the article.

David was on his second marriage, to the sister of his first wife, and apparently they all got along during the holidays. Compared to Peter and Neal, one could say David's life was more normal, but his approach to life was as Hunter S. Thompson it gets. Whether he was logging hours at his straight job in publishing, working on pro bono cases for artists, or speaking at political functions he would be high as a kite with an interesting twist on the facts that won people over.

Leaving The Bagel, I thought how beautifully interesting and broken humanity is.

Chapter Seventeen

In the fall of 1993 Nathan, Rose, Garrett and I gathered at the Receiving Department. Nathan had ordered dinner and set up a dining table. He made it look elegant with some help from the lighting and a theatrical props rental house. We were surrounded by crates of weed and bundles of cash, but the table laid out was first class with candlesticks and fancy stemware.

We were selling almost 500 pounds per week and I was delivering more than a hundred million per year to Robert. We had laundered something like a half billion dollars over the last five years—not enough to create an industry, but enough to light a spark and add a little excitement. The growers had made plenty of money from the herb sales, and so far only a little more from their above-board investments, but they were thrilled to have so much clean money. Some even considered retiring.

"To our apparent success," toasted Nathan. As we clinked glasses, he looked each of us in the eyes. "I want to thank you for taking this incredible ride and handling all the challenges smoothly. I toast each one of you."

Nathan topped off our glasses and continued, "It is a little hard to keep track of where this is going and if our milestones are leading us in the right direction. Surely the weed business is an incredible success on its own, and we have certainly routed a lot of money toward our bigger agenda, but it is still hard to gauge our effectiveness. On our most clandestine front I have asked Garrett to come to our bunker and give us an update. To bring it down to dollars and cents, the account that we all have been contributing to for Garrett's operation has had almost $40 million go through it over the last few years and I am wondering if that money has been well spent."

I was hoping this wouldn't become a boring presentation of return on investment and crossed my fingers, hoping no one was going to pull out spreadsheets. Nathan had arranged takeout from Basta Pasta and it smelled great. Rose was sitting across from me and looked hot. I am not sure if she dressed for us, but she was in an evening gown that showed off her cleavage and she wasn't wearing a wig, which made her neckline very inviting. My preference for my first bite would have been into the sinews of her neck where it meets her shoulder.

I was in it for the adventure and the punk ethos of fucking with the system, I didn't care so much for the details, but I was part of the gang so I steeled myself for a data dump that would certainly take the charm out of the meal. Luckily, Garrett was riding high on a deep draft of the internet Kool-Aid and his body language alone was entertaining. He wasn't going to give us a profit and loss statement; he was going to share the mead and allow us to look through his lens.

"The bunker has become a hub for the emerging cyberculture, both straight engineers and rabble-rousing hackers. We moved our internal operations, the stuff we don't talk about, upstairs, and the downstairs has become a shared work area where internet related start-ups can use workspace, common areas and access points at a very low cost, thanks to you. It is pretty exciting, actually; it feels like Haight Ashbury without the drugs, well, mostly.

"The political fight has been the most interesting. Right when we started back in '88, we pushed to get the government to understand the infrastructure required for a global internet. Some very well-respected professors from UCLA presented a paper to the Senate and must have brought some weed with them because a few senators joined the crusade and started singing the gospel right away. It took a few years, but the Gore bill suggested a framework that all parties could use to build infrastructure that is technologically neutral across all hardware and platforms. Perhaps more importantly, it funded some think tanks around the country and we did our best to make sure certain locations looked more attractive than others

"The rub between upstairs and downstairs is dramatic. They are well siloed, but I am running up and down the stairs building and breaking the same thing."

With that he stopped talking and started eating. The three of us had cleaned our plates while he was talking and were enjoying the full-belly narcotic effect so it was quiet while he ate.

"So it is working? All the money is doing what you had hoped?" I asked.

"Simple answer, yes. Not so simple answer, I hope so."

Rose chimed in. "I see some of the startups in your petri dish are retail operations. I thought you were against any consumerism on the Web?"

"I was and still am, but also see such a development as unavoidable. By working with such entities I hope to maintain a view of the potential challenges that will arise in terms of misuse of data."

I saw a little smile come from Nathan. He was telling me that he was right again.

"Good, I am satisfied. Keep up the good work." I didn't want to belittle Garrett's efforts, but I didn't understand most of what he was implying and even if he got into the nitty gritty and laid it out for me, I am still not sure I would have understood. I was certainly proud of what we were doing, even if I had no desire to understand the details. We were changing the world for the better. We were building the groundwork for the next century. And in numerous ways we were fucking with the man to do it.

"So are there any next steps? Or do we keep up the routine of making tons of money and spending it as fast as we can?" I asked.

"We stay the course. A few more years and we will have a better sense of where this is going. I read a few weeks ago that NASA was considering building a website so they could have an internet presence. The smartest fucking guys on the planet, actual rocket scientists, are still deciding if NASA needs presence on the Web. Either they aren't so smart, or we are wrong. I don't know how far off the tipping point is, but we have to keep pursuing our goal," Nathan said as he poured the last of the wine into his glass.

I had a bit of a wine buzz and was adding a fatty to the mix. Rose was looking really good. I wondered if she had ever slept with Garrett.

"Where you off to tonight looking so fly?" I asked her between tokes.

"Nowhere. I dressed up for you boys. Is it not appreciated?"

We all agreed that we appreciated it. It made our meeting seem more formal.

"Will you walk me to a cab?" she asked me.

"Sure, let me get the cash out of my backpack."

We had a big old safe where we kept the money. It wasn't fancy, but it would slow someone down if we were robbed. There was a clipboard where I wrote the dollar amount, date and my initials.

"You are looking at me as if I am dessert," said Rose as we walked down the street arm in arm.

"You are looking pretty sweet."

"I'll tell you what. I am feeling a bit tired and certainly not creative, so how about you come over to my place and eat me for an hour. Then you can masturbate and cum on my chest?"

She said it half-jokingly, but she knew I would do almost anything for her, and she wasn't asking anything I wasn't very excited to do.

Her apartment was an over-sized one-bedroom in a

brownstone on 10th Street. Big windows faced south and she had gauzy drapes in front of them that let the light through but obscured vision. She was a collector of sorts in that she collected what she liked. She was always ducking into secondhand shops, artisan boutiques, pawn shops and anyplace that might have something unique. She did the same when she traveled to other countries. Her things and the decorative elements didn't match in color, style, age or any factor I could recognize, but it came together in a very chic and organized interior.

There was a plate of glass held up by three pyramids that acted as a coffee table. The couch was black leather, but didn't dominate the room as the rug was white and the walls were muted whites that had different pastel tints. Her dining table was modern Scandinavian design, but the chairs were mid-century American. I never saw her cook, but the pots that were visible were all copper-bottomed and looked to have been handmade. She had a variety of lamps; one had a large gaudy base that was an Elizabethan scene of two suitors addressing a wallflower. If I saw it on its own, I would have suggested smashing it so it wouldn't offend anyone else, but in the cornucopia of design genres she had going, it fit right in.

The bedroom had a king-size bed that was a custom, built-in affair that was dark walnut and the bedding was all rich, thick cotton. That was where I headed.

I took off most of my clothes and waited for her to join me. She said she wanted to take a shower and proceeded to do a sexy strip tease in front of me. It wasn't the type you would see at a strip club, all focused on body parts, though she certainly had no shame about her nakedness. She understood sexuality and knew how to work her own sultriness into a riveting performance. If what you see at a strip club can be compared to most of the porn you see, I would say her display was more film noir. She got in my head, pushed my insecurity buttons, then strengthened me, pulled my attention into her satisfaction, then pushed it back to my growing need, made me want more, then overwhelmed me. It probably wasn't that long, but it felt like a whole opera that went through different perspectives and emotions. Her shower seemed to take forever.

I don't think I lasted an hour between her legs, but she rocked and rolled and squeezed my head, then pushed me down and moved her sex over my mouth, staring me in the eyes while my tongue marathoned on. At some point she came so hard that she pushed me out of the way and said she couldn't take it anymore. After catching her breath she started to massage her chest and pinch her nipples while talking in a sultry voice, pushing me to show my excitement for her. Her voice was so sexy as she moaned about how much she loved my tongue and how hot I looked holding myself and jerking for her. Then she started to tease me about how much I wanted to be inside her. When she moved her hands down and opened herself, I lost it. After convulsing I fell on the bed and held her until her breathing calmed and I could tell she was asleep. With one more look at her sexy body I covered her with the blanket and let myself out.

Chapter Eighteen

Marteen was a class-A freak. She dressed almost exclusively in '70s throwback sweatsuits, all orange and the fuzzier the better. An avid roller-skater, she was nearly always in skates and was so smooth on them that she wore them all day, up and down stairs, in and out of stores and restaurants. She had an African-American ancestor a few generations back, and looked whiter than half of Europeans, but her identity was completely wrapped up in being a downtrodden soul sister. She listened to reggae and urban music and only slept with black guys, though she wasn't picky about the race of chicks she was with. Her speech was like an old dread you might meet on a beach in Jamaica. She talked shit like she was from the ghetto, but she had been adopted by a wealthy family and grew up in Short Hills, New Jersey, a snobby, upscale suburb of New York City. She never felt like she fit in, especially in high school, so she split when she was 16 and followed manifest destiny.

She orbited the Bay Area for a few years and, through the Grateful Dead grapevine, met some major players in the biz. When she moved back to New York City, she had some great connections, both buying and selling. When we met on tour, we were both aging teenagers and slinging the Mexican money-making weed. We could basically get the same price so we didn't do much business, only occasionally when one of us couldn't get a load and had to fill an order. When the Cali plan went into effect she jumped right in and became one of my biggest customers. She was also one of the few people in my extended social network who knew not only that I was in the biz, but to what extent I was involved.

In the early '90s there was a restaurant on Grove Street that was taken over by some guys my age and they served great food in a relaxed environment. Its biggest draw was the garden in the back that opened onto Grove Street. The owners were smokers and didn't care if people smoked in the garden once it was down to regulars. The waitstaff was mid-twenty-year-olds, mostly from out-of-town, many of whom were pursuing acting careers. Besides being fun to party with, they were also pretty dialed into what was happening on any night of the week. It became a pretty reliable social hub that a bunch of us cycled through. I had one traveling musician friend who had to call first to find out who was on shift because he had slept with a few of the waitresses.

Finding Marteen eating alone at the bar, with her skates on, I asked her to join me and we got a table in the garden. The tables were old school desks, probably meant for one student as there was only one inkwell, but were comfortable as a four top, and a few round tables for two. Most of the tables were empty. Marteen deftly negotiated the wood floor, and the tile floor and the gravel in the garden in her skates without spilling her drink.

"Yo, you believe that shit. Whitey talked mad shit about legalizing weed and now he be all up in the oval not talking shit. During the election, nigger's on *Saturday Night Live* blowin' some bullshit like he of the people. Just when we think we got rid of the warmongering, bull-shitting, misogynist, racist and classist motherfuckers, we come to find it just the same old same old. Even if he didn't become a corporate bitch during the election, whatever fire-breathing lizard freak they got underneath the White House breathed his juju and flipped the script on us."

She paused to drink her wine. Slowly setting the glass down she looked at me and asked, "What worse? That they play us, or that we let ourselves get played?"

The waitress interrupted us to take my order. One nice thing about being a regular is not having to suffer embarrassment at my ordering style. I liked a pint of seltzer with half a lemon, and I ate a lot. It was not uncommon for me to order a couple of appetizers and entrees and I was tired of the response I got at restaurants where they didn't know me.

"I'll have the soup, the goat cheese salad, the swordfish and the hanger steak, medium." I just got my order out before an ambulance got stuck on Grove Street and its siren owned the airwaves until it could get past.

"Nuclear war, nuclear waste, global warming, droughts, fucking bullshit politicians making our lives worse, don't seem like anything is getting better."

"You got to stop thinking about all that, it will make you crazy."

"Funny thing, everywhere I look it all bad. I read, talk to people, keep my eyes and ears open and except for some kitten rescued from a tree that always makes its way to the news, shit is bad. Yet, it don't bring me down. I don't know how I can feel so hopeful. I think I have an irrational propensity toward joy. Weed help make it irie, but there is more. I buggin' out on it wondrin' I crazy. So much bullshit in the world, how I get off on thinking it gonna be aaeeght?

"I see a bum on the street the other day and I tried to buy him a pair of shoes; 'is shoes was all worn out. Otherwise he look pretty clean. He was insulted. Imagine that. My heart go out to him and I want to help and he was embarrassed like I pity him. I just riding high and felt like helping. Cheap satisfaction, I know, but fuck it, dude needed a pair of shoes."

"Was he crazy?"

"Ain't we all? He wasn't all talkin' to himself and shit, but he for sure living on the street, so I guess he a little bit cracked."

The garden had cleared out when my food started arriving and Marteen rolled a joint and proceeded to smoke it by herself while I ate in silence. I was thinking how easy it is to give and how little is given. How often does pride prevent someone from receiving a pair of shoes? Buddhists speak of seven kinds of pride, including thinking someone is better than you. Are those not included in the multitude of have-nots really stingy? Or are they respecting social barriers thrown out there by those who would benefit from spontaneous generosity? Giving so effectively strokes one's ego; it is hard to imagine there isn't more giving. Looking at Marteen I couldn't imagine anyone thinking she was anything but about peace and love.

"We have to stop waiting for the government to solve our problems and do it ourselves. I read that the NRA, the Boy Scouts and the Sierra Club were teaching kids upstate how to hunt because there aren't enough hunters. Can you imagine three orgs with such diverse interests coming together to solve a problem where their mandates overlap?"

I continued, "The history of political animals, herds, hives, humans, et al., is the story of an imposition of hierarchical power upon those who lacked strength or resources. Some charismatic personality or dogma has always been at the peak of a top-down ordering of society. Of course we can see the threats and challenges of survival that drove us to this point in our social evolution, but it was always driven by scarcity of resources. What if there were smaller groups of people with similar interests and objectives and specific mandates came together with other groups when the mandates overlapped and need arose? Government would be out of business.

" Charlie and Freddy had it right: utopic ideas are on hold until we reach that tipping point. One day we will realize everyone has had breakfast and we can all climb Maslow's Pyramid together singing 'Kumbaya.'"

"What about all the white men who be holding all dat money?"

"Let them keep it. They can breed and educate and even gate themselves off. What harm? Like artists who commit their life to art, one could commit their life to financial pursuits if that suited their temperament. I mean, we need those people just like we need farmers and carpenters, though we may end up with less use for lawyers. And we need focused resources to do stuff. It costs a lot of money to build a bridge or a factory to build solar panels. Let them gather their shekels so that great artists and dreamers may have funding to bring forth their visions. And forget about noblesse oblige; if everyone can eat and live safely, who cares how many possessions another may have?"

"You think any real change gonna come without cracking heads? People getting fed up with dis bullshit. Ghetto's been quiet for a minute now, but one spark and cities will be burning."

"I think the change is inevitable barring some extinction-level event. It won't require any catalyst or force. I have a lot of faith in the goodness of humanity, but after the honeymoon is over, we will really find out if we can let go of fear."

"What happened to 'Kumbaya'?"asked Deanna, our waitress, who once off-shift had brought a round of drinks and joined our party with one of the owners.

"How does it work if organizations come together to solve a problem and there is a problem with the solution? What if a problem comes up and there is no immediate authority to handle the problem? How responsive can such a system be? And of course there will always be bullies on the playground who want power over others. How do we deal with them? Will that ugly slice of human nature fall away with the all-consuming pursuit of stuff? I am not so sure."

"There will always be assholes," stated Stan, who was the bigger asshole of the two owners. "And most people will always want more. I disagree that we are driven by concern over our next meal. People want to feel they are better than others."

"So you are saying," asked Deanna, "instead of food,

clothing and shelter for all, we might do better providing therapy so they can get over their insecurities?"

"Maybe, but it is as realistic as what he is suggesting. Human nature is so ingrained in our DNA that it would take geological time to see any difference in how we relate to each other," added Stan.

"You may be right, but we won't find out until the system starts to change to reflect the realization that feeding everyone won't take any food off anyone's plate."

"Yeah, whatev, whatev. Some smooth-talking snake oil salesman always gonna be working the room selling some dream and whipping people up into a frenzy. Come to find out the salesman the only one makin' out, but the people won't care. They follow the words of whoever has the silverest tongue."

"It is hard to envision due to the transformative potential of the death of scarcity. I hear you, Stan, that there are other motivations. But it is impossible to tell the depth of the effect that living with want on a life-or-death level has had on our desires and emotions. It is hard to get out of the mindset of scarcity and consider what our pro-social motivations might become once freed from concerns like strife and hunger at the beginning and end of life, or the basic fears of a mother bringing a new life into the world."

"Yeah, it is easy for you to be an optimist because you aren't suffering. Everybody else thinks we are going to hell in a bucket, and quick," said Stan, in an attacking tone.

I was used to people reacting strongly to my vision of a peaceful future. Sometimes they got mad, sometimes they smiled, thinking I was nuts, and let me ramble without trying to hear what I was saying. Of course I can't be right; it hasn't happened yet. But I might be right and such a world will require all our optimism to blossom.

Marteen and I left Grove and headed toward Stringfellows, an upscale strip club in the 20s. Marteen wanted to have a few more drinks and look at beautiful women's bodies before we headed to Nells for the late-night scene. I had to tip the doorman to get in because I wasn't wearing a suit and on weeknights it is all about the business crowd. It didn't hurt that I was with a woman either.

We sat down in the oversized, plush chairs at a table in the corner where we could see the whole room and all the stages. The cocktail waitress came over and took our drink order. As she was leaving, she stopped and turned to me and called me by my name. She looked sort of familiar, but I couldn't have placed her. Turns out Sara was a year younger than me at Bronx Science and had developed a bit of a crush on me. We chatted a bit when she brought our drinks, then I saw her pointing me out to a few of her fellow employees. One was Cindy, who had just moved to New York City from Missouri and didn't know anybody in town. I guess whatever Sara told her made her curious and she took over our table. She was hot and I asked her why she wasn't dancing, as she would certainly make more money. The blush of innocence that swept over her face was captivating as she explained why she wasn't into dancing. Like a virgin in a harem, what could be sexier than that? Marteen caught it and she said it made her wet.

At around 1:30 we were getting ready to leave and Cindy asked if she could join us. As the newest waitress, she was cut loose first when the crowd started to thin. Marteen and I both said, "Sure."

We walked the few blocks arm in arm in arm, with Cindy in the middle. I had never seen Marteen put the moves on a woman before. She blended masculine and feminine sensuality in her seduction and I thought for sure I had lost out.

Clubs go through different phases in New York City. They usually start very exclusively, known only by word of mouth. At this phase there are velvet ropes, but not much of a line. People either don't know about it or know they can't get in. Area was the only club I knew of that maintained this phase for its entirety. Nells had zoomed through that phase, went bridge-and-tunnel, had a resurgence of exclusivity and famous faces, became almost a local bar, resurged again with a dance crowd and now was basically a place for white women to hook up with black dudes. It was perfect for Marteen, who ditched us as soon as we had our first drink. I saw her throughout the night riding up on brothers on the dance floor and in the dark corners. She was probably shopping for the biggest package.

That left me alone with Cindy. I couldn't imagine how little experience she had. She lived with her sister and in the six months she had been living in town she had only a couple of dates that left her dry. Her problem was she wanted to taste the high life, but she couldn't find an entrance. Held back by fear, innocence, and some Midwest morality, she was hoping to find an accomplice so she could dip her toes or swim in the water while feeling safe. All the dates she had were with suits that didn't have any sense of adventure. She told me of one guy she had slept with a few times. She had asked him to tie her up and basically had to show him how to do it.

I was a bit torn. I am pretty kinky, but wasn't sure I wanted to be responsible for sending her down that road. In my mind I saw myself taking her in front of a crowd while hot wax was being dripped on her nipples, and such a club was only a few blocks away. I wondered if anybody had ever smacked her ass? Would she come when spanked? Another part of my brain went to a more romantic, missionary relationship where we dated and went to movies and plays and I never fucked her in the ass or had her give me a blowjob in public. My experience with Cindy showed me how little my plans matter when the chick is in heat.

Her sister's house was a few blocks from my apartment and I walked her home. It was four in the morning when I left her at her door. I gave her my phone number and said she should call if she wanted to go out again and I split. I was so oversexed in my brain I had to jerk off before going to bed. Images danced in my head: the dancers with augmented sexiness, Marteen working Cindy, then working the black dudes in the club, Cindy's innocence and hot body. It didn't take long before I was asleep.

I slept until noon. While in the shower I heard Cindy's voice on the answering machine. "That was quick," I thought, wondering how I should play this one. She was six or seven years younger than me, with very little experience. I figured I would be chivalrous and work her socially until she overcame her fears and jumped me. After that we would play it by ear.

I got dressed and went down to the Receiving Department. I had a couple of deliveries to make and would be in and out all day. First was Kiki. He had a new apartment in Chinatown that overlooked the east river. When I arrived with 50 pounds, I noticed some Gumbas standing around outside the building. I knew he worked with people I wouldn't work with, but he was from the hood and seemed to have it under control. Kiki was Italian and had grown up in Soho. He was a bit shy as a boy so his dad threw him in a boxing school to toughen him up. The school was in the basement of a church on Bleecker Street and though the coach's intentions were pro-social, it turned out a lot of boys ready and willing to act as muscle for the local social clubs (all the mob groups had storefronts in Little Italy). My sixth sense told me to keep walking, but I figured if they were there for Kiki they already knew who I was. I said hello to the gents, who pretended not to notice me.

"Dude, what's up? You have some unfriendlies hovering around your door downstairs, they for you?"

"Yeah, and you."

"What the fuck, dude?"

Just then the door opened and in walked an older Italian gentleman in an overcoat and a hat followed by two of the guys who had been downstairs. Everybody knew Mr. G. and I guess I should have been honored to have a one-on-one with him. One of the muscle heads took his coat and hat and the two of them stood on either side of the door outside the apartment and closed the door.

"Kiki has told me about you and your supply. Seems I don't know everything about shipments in and out of New York City. I am supposed to know everything."

I looked at Kiki with a silent, "What the fuck, dude?"

"Get him up to speed, I have to take a piss."

"I lost a trip these guys had put money in. I had a truck from Arizona stopped in Tennessee and lost the load. The driver is stand-up, so I am not worried about legal implications, but Mr. G. here thinks of the shipment as being guaranteed by me and didn't understand when I explained it was a shared risk. They want their money, which I don't have because I had most of my cash invested in the load."

"What the fuck does that have to do with me?"

"I had been selling them some of the kind bud as well and they said if I introduced them to my connection they wouldn't fuck with me." He paused and looked me right in the eyes, "Or my people."

"Fuck!" I mouthed silently. I had always avoided family ties. Too unpredictable and into too many different hustles. And most importantly, violence. I liked working with hippies and do-gooders who thought as much about saving the world as they did about making a buck. The family guys were always about the money, and now in their eyes, Kiki owed them.

Mr. G. came out of the bathroom while zipping his pants. He sat down opposite me, relaxed into the chair and stared at me. The silence was uncomfortable as we, like wild animals, sized each other up. I knew all about him, having grown up in the neighborhood, but I was a curiosity for him. I am sure Kiki had told him I wasn't into guns or tough-guy shit and perhaps he thought intimidation would be the way to go. I did my best to convince him otherwise. To help Kiki I would consider business arrangements, but if he went for straight-up extortion it would put my pacifism to the test. While staring into his eyes I imagined going commando and killing him, his family and his whole organization.

"So, you have a pretty good supply. How are you getting it into town?"

I just stared at him, trying to think happy murderous thoughts while swallowing my fear during another uncomfortable pause.

"Look, Kiki has put us in an awkward situation and we are just looking for a way to make it better."

Holding his stare, I said, "There are no guarantees in this business and we have all lost loads before."

I could tell Kiki was getting nervous. I am pretty sure he wanted to tell me how close I was to some serious danger. I don't know what he expected from me, but a hippie playing tough was definitely a surprise.

"You know me and my friends usually know all the angles. We have been selling drugs since before your parents were born, besides other shit, and I want to understand how something this big can be happening under our noses. And I am not talking about just the quantity; more than a few people noticed the Cisco IPO after weed of the same name was all over town."

I don't know where it comes from. Most of the time I run from trouble, but sometimes my instincts tell me there is no place to run and I stand. "You know the problem with your organization is you make too much noise and too many enemies. I would never work with you because some youngin in your crew will do something stupid and bring your whole game down. Or the feds will come down on the docks, or gambling, or prostitution or any of the other hustles you have going and take a good thing down. The difference between you and me is you would do anything to make a buck. I supply a product that everybody wants and does no one harm. You are too old and bloated to change when markets change. I mean, really, hanging on to the Mex game when the writing's on the wall."

Mr G. looked amused and made no attempt to interrupt me.

"You are so exposed on so many levels that a pebble tossed in your pond would become a tsunami. Don't get me wrong, I appreciate everything you are doing as it is a great smoke screen for the rest of us. You are into all the stupid shit that makes for good news stories and walk around with a great big target on your back. I am nobody doing something that doesn't raise an eyebrow unless a truck falls into the cops' lap."

"So we have nothing to talk about?"

"You seem to have a problem with my friend; I will talk about that." I leaned forward in my chair as I said it. It was so comical that Mr. G. laughed. Not so much at me, but at the situation. I was trying to use body language to play it tough with the toughest guy around, someone who with a nod of his head can rack up a body count.

"It's all funny until someone goes to the morgue or jail," I said, playing through. "I don't see how Kiki owes you anything, certainly not an introduction."

"So we should just forget about our money?"

"I know Kiki would not have personally guaranteed your money; you can't do that with all the shit that goes on. My guess is you know that already and are trying to get in on the action because you put on your glasses to read the writing on the wall. Kiki has a lot of respect for you but that is some bullshit."

"You fucking think you know what the fuck is happening here? I will tell you what is happening here; you are our new fucking supplier whether you like it or not. I don't give a shit about a half a million dollars compared to the potential here. And I am really curious about the money trail after it leaves your hands."

I got up. "I am done here. You lost your money and have a connection. If you want to buy the kind you can talk to Kiki; there is 50 pounds there. If you have a problem with that fuck you."

I turned to Kiki and told him I would see him next week. I didn't know what would happen next, but I figured leaving the 50 pounds might chill things out. I opened the door to leave and Mr. G. waved to the muscle to let me by.

My heart was racing. I tried to control my breathing as I walked across Canal Street. I did more of a duck-and-weave than normal. Jumping on a bus, going in and out of the subway from different angles, window shopping to see if I was being followed, the whole time trying to think of a way out of the mess I was in. Certainly I had to move, or leave town, or country. I wondered if I handled it right. It felt good, but maybe I hadn't taken the time to consider the long-term play. I am fucked, was all I could think.

Nathan was at the Receiving Department when I arrived. He sensed my agitation and I told him the whole story. He reassured me that I did the right thing.

"That is all they understand. If you had flinched or shown fear, he would have eaten you alive. Now he is probably wondering if you are crazy or if you can back up your attitude. He isn't the first person to connect the dots with Cisco either. He is probably more interested in cleaning his money than selling more drugs. Let me see what I can do. Can you meet me back here in a few hours, say 6 o'clock?"

"Sure, I have a run to make; I will come back then."

"Alright, be careful. Mr. G. is a businessman, so he is not likely to do anything right away, but it is safe to say you definitely didn't make a friend."

Chapter Nineteen

"You are right," said Marteen. "You are fucked."

She was my next stop and while smoking a joint I had told her what had happened with Mr. G. Marteen lived in the Archive building on Christopher Street, which had recently been renovated, again, and was now high-end rentals. It was a big space, but felt odd as it was so long it felt narrow, and the only windows were all the way at one end. I also didn't like the doorman aspect of my coming and going, but Marteen assured me the building was busy with all sorts of work-at-home entrepreneurs and no one would notice. It was also comforting to know that she didn't bring many people into her home. She delivered to most of her customers and because she had a legit business in Anguilla that she used as a smoke screen, her friends and lovers had no idea she was in the weed biz.

"I don't think they will whack me for my attitude, but I don't think I have heard the last of it. He seemed more interested in the operation than the product."

"I got questions too, but I figure if you want to share you will."

"What do you mean?"

"My peeps in the Bay Area be complaining about all the weed being bought by out-of-staters. With the rents skyrocketing in San Francisco they need to make bank, but the growers in Humboldt selling their whole trip in one shot and here you got mad shipments coming into New York City. I also ran into your boy Robert at the Shoreline shows. He all with the straight job and shit, but he been hanging with you a bunch more than makes sense. Makes me wonder why you be spending so much time in Sacramento."

"That story might be a few more years before the telling."

"Word, I guess that. Cool with me, just watch yourself."

"Yeah," I said, exhaling, relaxing my lungs to let the smoke out as I fell back into the chair.

"What up with the hottie from the Midwest?"

"She called already. I am going to hook up with her tomorrow, daytime. I wonder what she looks like without the strip club makeup."

"That girl ready to be turned out. So sexy to see someone so inexperienced yet so curious and adventurous standing on the precipice. You gonna push her over?"

"Funny, part of me wants to fulfill my teenage romance fantasy, all flowers and poetry. Another part of me wants to take her to the dark side. We shall see."

"Good luck with that, and if you want to share…"

We hugged and I left. I went to the Odeon for a late lunch while I tried to think of a plan to deal with the mobsters I had so brazenly faced off. After eating I went to the Receiving Department and waited in silence for Nathan. Where did he go? What could he do to help besides taking out a mob boss?

"All sorted," he said as he walked in. Nathan, always sure of himself, was that plus some. He was beaming as if he had just actually pulled a rabbit out of a hat.

"What do you mean sorted?" I asked.

"I have to tell you this life is freakin' crazy. I thought I would ask my friend who works in the anti-racketeering department about this Mr. G. Turns out the guy is a rat working for the feds. It was the feds that put him up to turning the screws on you as they try and sniff out as many hustles as they can before they start making arrests."

"How does that help us, or more specifically me?"

"We just have to get word to the team running Mr. G. that you are off limits. I already made a call. It may get a little tricky down the line, but it buys us some time."

"Tricky...buys time?"

"One way to keep the heat off is to keep the heat on. If our operation is being investigated by anybody, everyone else will have to stay clear. Mr. G. didn't jump to conclusions on his own; he had some branch of the feds talking in his ear. If we have somebody else investigating us, then any information would have to flow through one office, which we could control for a while. Maybe Treasury. Anyway, that is a last resort. For now I think we are safe from Mr. G. and I doubt any of his friends or competitors know about you. You had better get to Kiki and let him know we are sorted. Don't tell him how, just that it is done."

"Wow, what a fucking day. I am going to meet with Kiki and then get drunk and pass out." I touched Nathan on his arm and looked in his eyes and said, "Thanks, man."

"No problem. I will see you in a couple of weeks. Cheers."

Kiki and I met at a dive bar on the East Side, the Holiday Lounge. I think the Holiday holds the record for most overdoses in a bar. They served cheap beer from a dirty bar and the patrons looked like they had dressed as horror film extras 10 years ago and hadn't bothered taking a shower since.

"What do you mean we are good?"

"I mean we are good. Mr. G. accepted the terms of our offer. You don't owe him anything and his crew will still buy from you."

"Our offer? Is that what you call it? I thought you were trying to get yourself killed."

"To be honest I surprised myself. I mean, as I heard the words come out of my mouth I was shocked at my stupidity and bravado, and wondered who the fuck was talking." I paused for a pull from my pint. "Fuck it, it worked out fine, we are good. I just convinced him that I might just be a kind of crazy he doesn't want to deal with. Survival instincts will lead us to accept some strange deals in life."

"You are fucking crazy, dude. I thought for sure we were

both dying right in my new apartment." He took a swig of his beer and put his hand on my shoulder. "And hey man, really, I am sorry."

"Don't worry, we dealt with it and it probably strengthened your position as well. I am sure they still want you out of the way, but now it is clear you are a necessary nuisance. And with that I am out of here."

I downed my beer and headed for the door. The Gap had moved into St. Marks and there was a serious attempt to put a clean, safe, happy face on the neighborhood, but the neighborhood resisted. Even as rents went up, the streets were still dirty and the bars still divey. That was part of the attraction for the newcomers, who tripped over the detritus of nightlife on their way to their day job. They were cool; they lived on the Lower East Side.

I had nowhere to be and I felt like I had been on an emotional yo-yo ride. I hopped in a cab and went uptown to the Madison Hotel, which had a great spa where the women walk on you. I loved it when they dug their heels between my shoulder blades and rocked back and forth. After getting two massages with steam, sauna and ice plunge in between, I was done. I skipped dinner and slept for 12 hours.

When I met Cindy, she wasn't wearing any makeup and was looking quite comfortable in her overalls. She wasn't right off the bus; she was right off the hay wagon. She wielded a big smile that can only be learned in the fly-over states and was as Ivory clean as one could be. I rolled with freaks and intellectuals and was wondering what I had gotten myself into.

She came up to me and, as if she was happy to finally have a friend, put her arm through mine and asked, "What should we do?"

"Are you hungry?"

"No."

"How about a museum?"

"Sure, where should we go, city boy?"

"How about MoMA? They have a show about mutant materials in modern manufacturing, though I think the name of the show doesn't actually hit the alliteration button that heavy."

"You are funny."

The overalls did it. She looked both completely out of place and completely at ease. I felt like I was with a brand-new spirit seeing the world for the first time. She laughed at my jokes, gave me a little slap when my sarcasm felt impolite to her, and was generally amazed at everything. She seemed to flutter like a butterfly around all the sophisticates in the museum, but she didn't miss a thing. She had some deep frontier wisdom about her that wasn't quite the same as street smarts or knowledge, but came from a thoughtful combination of curiosity, patience and common sense.

We had lunch afterward at the China Grill, which was definitely the finest restaurant she had ever been in. As we ate, I could tell she wanted me. She was looking for a boyfriend who could show her the town and I was ringing all her bells. I had money and she was attracted to my roughness. She could sense danger and excitement and she wanted to taste it, to lick it off my neck.

It was fun to watch her screw up her courage. We were sitting next to each other, which presented closeness, but also the awkwardness of not facing each other. She touched me as often as conversation presented an opportunity. On my hand, my leg. At one point I mentioned my dog when I was a kid and she caressed my cheek in condolence. She sipped her wine while holding my gaze with the sexiest little pout she could muster. I knew as we left that she wasn't going to let me out of her sight until we had made love.

On our way downtown I pointed out a few sights, including taking her into the Algonquin Hotel to show the round table where New York luminaries had gathered. She mentioned that it was a really nice hotel.

"Should we get a room?"

"Definitely!"

When we got in the room I flopped on the bed and asked what we should do now. I watched her face move from frustration to self-doubt to seize-the-moment. She realized I was going to make her lead and she gathered up her belle charm and walked over to the bed.

"We should start with these," she said as she took off my shoes and socks.

"Then this," as she took off my shirt.

She was so fucking sweet. She was going for it, and in such a non-pretentious and present way. I could tell she was nervous and that added to the excitement. She brushed her lips against mine as I fought the urge to grab her and run her over. She kissed me lightly a few times, then held her lips to mine as she explored my mouth with her tongue. She caressed my head and grabbed my neck and pulled me into a deep kiss. She was even a little rough as she explored a strength, a power inside herself that she had never known was there.

She kissed her way down to my belly and looked up at me. "And what about these?" she asked as she bit on my waistband.

"I don't know, this is our first date."

"Oh, sure, like you are going to refuse this?" she asked as she unbuckled her overalls and pulled off her top. She wasn't wearing a bra, and didn't need one, and she did a slow reveal as the shirt came off. They were perfect, like two snow-covered volcanoes. Her belly was flat and confirmed the workout routine she had alluded to.

As her arms came down her hand went right to my crotch. It wasn't difficult for her to find what she was looking for. My hardness assured her of her desirability.

"Now are you going to make me do all the work?"

"This first time, yes ma'am. I am."

Her courage faltered and then recovered. She could tell that I was relaxed and willing to be present through her exploring her sexuality with no judgment. She took off my pants and took me in her mouth. She was so gentle and welcoming and she used all her senses trying to get to know me, even rubbing me against her ears. She worked on me for a while and then looked up and asked if she was doing something wrong.

"Definitely not. I am in heaven. Why would you ask?"

"Most guys come pretty quick after I show them my tits and take them in my mouth. I kept my virginity until I was 20 that way."

"No reflection on your talents here. I like to take my time."

"You sure?"

"Absolutely, now if you are done talking…"

She smiled and continued licking and kissing my hardness while looking in my eyes.

"You hadn't looked up before."

"I was embarrassed."

"You aren't now?"

"I feel really comfortable with you. Usually sex is wham bam, thank you ma'am. You say take your time; what does that mean?"

"Do you have plans tonight?"

"No."

"Good, we aren't putting on clothes until the morning."

"Can we order room service?" she asked hopefully, like it was her first time.

"Of course."

At the moment I was the meal and she went at it with increased enthusiasm. She sucked and tickled and stared until she said, "I need you inside me, now."

"Help yourself," I said, and she did.

Her little hands guided me inside her as she sank down on

top of me. She worked it until she had taken all there was to take. She started rocking, but I stopped her.

"Just stay there for a minute, don't move."

She became more accustomed to me being inside her and I flexed a few times to give her a rush. I could feel her getting very wet around me. Then she started a slow-motion back-and-forth as if I wouldn't notice—tiny movements with increased intensity as she stared in my eyes. Then she started to lose focus and the blinks became longer until her eyes were closed and she was rocking the bed, throwing me back-and-forth as her hips got a workout. Her face was angelic when she came, something not of this world, but pure and holy and without distortion. Human experience as divine as can be found flashed across her face.

She collapsed onto my chest and I bear-hugged her. She never calmed down because as soon as she caught her breath, she realized I was still hard inside of her.

"Oh my God, there's more?"

"Take your time, or we can take a break. That was beautiful. Thank you for sharing your sexuality with me," I said as I kissed her face. "Should I roll a joint?"

"Perfect, but you have to do it staying inside of me."

We played adult Twister as we got to my pants and retrieved my stash and rolling papers. We smoked and fucked, her always on top all night. The only interruption was room service, which brought wine and dinner. We ate on the bed. After the wine was gone, I was once again inside of her. When room service came to clean up, I didn't allow her to move or cover up. The waiter saw the scene and was going to leave when I stopped him and assured him it was alright. I am sure he had seen all sorts of craziness working in the hotel. My pants were still in reach and I tipped him $50 for staring at my girl's tits. When he left, Cindy went nuts and rode me through either multiple orgasms or one 20-minute long orgasm. I wasn't not sure. Apparently public display was a hot button for her.

We fell asleep in each other's arms.

I woke up with the sunrise as we hadn't closed the blinds and ravaged her from behind. All the build-up of the night before exploded as I came over her back after a fierce quickie. Then I closed the blinds and we slept until they chased us out at noon. I walked her home and told her I was free in the evening.

At nine o'clock that night my cell phone rang and it was Cindy. Her sister was in show biz and some of her friends were gathering at a drag queen club around the corner from my house and she wanted to know if I wanted to go. The 5 Oaks had been around as long as I had a memory. There were performances most nights of the week that I could hear through the courtyard from my apartment. I was guaranteed to hear "It's Raining Men" and "I Will Survive" at least once a night. I assumed it was all lip-syncing but had never actually gone in. I passed, but said she could come to my house anytime.

She showed up a little tipsy and when we made love, I took control. She was like a finely tuned sex machine, and she was limber and light enough for me to lift into any position. She had a funny trait that she had obviously repressed in our first love session: she would come a couple of times and when she hit the big one she broke out laughing. Hysterical, choke-on-your-tongue kind of laughter. I had had girls cry before, but laughter was a new one for me. I couldn't help laughing too as she was unable to get control of herself. It definitely hit the pause button on the sex, but I was cool with that.

"I am so sorry," she said, "That happens sometimes."

"No need to apologize, that was awesome. I take it as a compliment."

"You don't think it is weird?"

"No."

We cuddled in silence for a while.

"I have to split town for a few days," I said.

"Where you going?"

"Out west."

"Can we make plans for when you get back?"

"Hmmm, I would have to check my schedule," I teased.

She hit me in the chest and I grabbed her and pinned her under my weight, which led us to finishing what we had started earlier. I was watching her rub my cum into her chest as I dozed off.

We became inseparable anytime I was in town. I didn't have a legal cover I could maintain so I told her I was involved with a delivery service for weed and nothing more. She actually became a great salesperson, always carrying a stack of business cards and a smile that assured a sense of trust.

It was the end of summer and time to get ready for harvest time and being bicoastal for a few months. I gathered all the cash I could get and headed back to Sacramento to meet with Robert.

JFK to Sacramento, rent a car, drive up north, drive south, SFO to Newark, repeat. Repeat. Business class helped, but you hear about bullet trains that could cross the country in six hours, not to mention all the modes of travel promised to us by sci-fi writers, and you realize air travel is pretty lame, especially since the 1993 World Trade Center bombing. That started the requirement of using ID at airports, not to mention to get into most buildings in Manhattan. It also moved security checkpoints to the front of the airport, which slowed things down. You could no longer go to the gates unless you had a ticket. There was a lot more inconvenience from security measures, but it didn't feel any safer.

Chapter Twenty

"The second movement is where the action happens, good or bad. The first movement creates a setting and introduces themes that build the story while characters are being introduced. Whether it be startling, calming or music for its own sake, its intent, its goal, is to present the senses with an understanding of where they are so the second movement can rally in on fertile ground. Sinister plots or happily-ever-after, it is only when the mystery is gone and the environment is mastered that the fates begin their meddling. Will the good guys win? Will true love reign? Will hope remain? The tension of not knowing is what makes a life more than a life, but a symphony. A libretto, not of disconnected points in one's emotional perception, however short or long in duration, but a life where individual abilities and that-which-makes-us-special are voiced in exquisite brushstrokes on a canvas that is undeniably one's own."

"Yes, but it is all just buying time until the third movement brings a resolution that leaves us afterwards with a very particular feeling. Until then the composer is just playing with our emotions. All that twisting and turning, contra this, contralto that. Really, they are just unabashedly ripping at our heartstrings, while our neck muscles constrict with anticipation and our tongues are gin-bender dry. I dare say I often read the last page first. Saves all that bother."

"I agree. One should pick a straight path and walk it. All this expression leads to nothing but more expression. Symphonies are such dramatic affairs. King Lear, Romeo, betrayal, true love and the rest, for what? Why must the hero leave town? Why do we need heroes anyway? What use is a canvas if you have to risk everything and introduce cacophony. The straight path is less fraught with atonal gibberish and falling on swords. Don't risk it. Keep to the well-tended, paved, rectilinear themes that offer the most satisfaction with the least risk. Paint landscapes, for Christ's sake. I mean really, trust the church. Did I mention I was going to be a minister?"

"I say not. The hero starts pure in the first act with great confidence that good instincts and good manners carve the story of a life, with convictions so well rooted they held all the way through the second act. Somewhere around the bassoon monologue you can see a shift. A crack. A delay in response that indicates perhaps all the answers are not possessed. A thought that perhaps some of those instincts brought a little banditry and roguish behavior. A canvas that started bold, a first movement of great glory enters the second movement with immediate discord. A reshuffling of ideals that introduce conflict, from nowhere sin and accountability become understood. Where once clear voices rang, now the timpani roll and thrum as the clarity sublimates and we are left wondering where we will find ourselves in the third act. The final movement, or is it?"

"Is it right to measure each bar and syllable with some emotion meter? Don't all symphonies have flaws? Aren't we all flawed? Is it over with the last note? The last word or stroke? Or is it over when we are nostalgic for moments of grace in some unknown beyond? Is it a good play? Is it a good character? Are the players even competent? Sometimes I think we all forgot to tune. A symphony, a life, a play should make us believe. What it is we believe should not be judged, but the depth of belief is an ample yardstick for the success of the endeavor."

"I say we have every right to base our opinions on the most auspicious phenomena in the tale. Surely there are missteps and a life is longer than the years would seem; how can a tab be kept? It is either the yardstick or peak moments, red or black in the register. You use whatever metric you desire, I for one am ready to make public my opinion of this canvas without further delay."

"Is that music for its own sake? Is there a major theme here at all? Were sins committed, has redemption been achieved? Can the story hold up with constant upheaval and reinvention? Is it to be judged on technical merits, if such a baseline could be agreed to? There has been no bloodshed, perhaps hearts ripped in two, but mostly smiles reflected in the wake. The work is more than technical. Great symphonies achieve more than direct experience. It leaves the community with a feeling of light and joy. Is that not the yardstick to use?"

I wasn't tripping. I was turning thirty years old and was asleep. One of those dreams that you know is a dream because it seems more real than reality. Apparently, I was the topic of conversation at this gathering of opinions. The people didn't look like themselves, but I could identify even the ones I didn't know. I remember when I was young it was easy to believe I could buy a picture book of symbols that would reveal all the depth of dreams and the subliminal world from which they drew their fodder. That was when I was twenty-eight. Or even twenty-nine and a half. Turning thirty seemed to be a beast, or a machine that leveled any previously held beliefs. Life was still a box of chocolates, but I now knew what it was like to have a belly ache.

I am not sure if the other personalities represented my patriarchs or amalgamations of various entertainment personalities. The message was clear. It was time to take stock. Usually that meant taking acid with a purpose. Turning thirty was epic; I wouldn't want the experience to be anything less than epic. I didn't feel the need to have a party; in fact I felt like being alone, in some place that captured how I felt, on top of the world.

Upon waking I opened the atlas to a view that centered on the North Pole. At 83 degrees north I found the northernmost airport with scheduled service in the town of Longyearbyen in the Norwegian island chain of Svalbard.

Landing in Longyearbyen as my 30th approached, I was ushered off the plane and across the tarmac to a small building that served as a terminal. Coming through the door we were all handed a small eight-page safety pamphlet whose cover showed a photograph of a polar bear eating a human, with the headline of "Take Polar Bear Danger Seriously." I stepped outside the terminal. There was not a tree or bush and hardly a blade of grass as far as the eye could see. The ground was covered in broken rock, and the whole terrain looked like an unsifted gravel basin. The airport faced the ocean, right where the long broad bay opened to the sea. The bay faced west and was perhaps three miles wide at its mouth and reached into the moonscape of an island for about four miles. I walked down to the shore, where the gentle waves lapped the broken ground, and watched a sailboat tacking as it made its way to the gaggle of boats at the top of the bay. I thought romantically, how for years the only way to reach these islands had been plying the winds and floating the Gulf Stream.

As I walked, I fantasized that after finding no hotel, I found passage on a ship to some exotic port. I would work for my berth and supper and let the music of the waves wash away the technocratic, cultural conditioning and leave a vestige of the archetypal ancient mariner. I was calling on foreign ports, dancing with the women, re-embarking to sail and singing with the dolphins. I had left my old self far behind when I reached the outskirts of town.

I asked around and found that there was a sixteen-room hotel at the top of the valley, and I was able to get a room. The hotel was a new addition and was one of the few buildings that used wood in its construction. The rooms were small and sparse, but offered panoramic views, and were quite comfortable with European charm. I got to my room, set my bag down, and went down to the bar.

I didn't get out of my room until two in the afternoon on my birthday. Breakfast and lunch were long over, so I bought some supplies at the commissary, both to have as breakfast and to carry on the hike I was planning. I had decided to hike to the highest point of the island, which was visible from town, at an elevation of four thousand feet. Being that it never got dark, it didn't matter that I was getting a late start. I packed a small bag with water, some food, and my Gortex shell. Then I retrieved some hot water from the bar to steep the hallucinogenic mushrooms I had brought and made myself a birthday tea. I sipped it slowly and looked at the awe-inspiring terrain out of my window. Killing time as I drank my tea, I opened the book on my nightstand. Like so many places, nighttime reading was supplied by a group of people named the Gideons, part of whose mission was to place a Bible by every bed. I was preparing to officiate at my brother's wedding, so I thought I would gather some notes for my oration. I needed to satisfy a diverse group at the wedding and thought I would mine the great book for some ideas.

This reading was to be unique. I had always enjoyed the stories and parables, the scripture deepening and supporting my own thoughts about the spiritual cosmology of the universe. But it had always been a separate entity, a chronicle of the past, and some tool used by the vast organization of the Church. But on this day, it lived. It breathed. The truths it held wound their way through my fingers, up my arms and into my brain and soul. The stories took on a greater meaning and the scripture poured forth like a visible wave issued forth from the trumpets of heaven. The angels danced, felt but unseen, in my room and the breath of creation filled my breast. I read, like a speed reader, not slowing down for the words, but drinking the meaning with the thirst of a desert traveler.

It was after nine o'clock when I finally put the book down. I passed, Cherubim like, out of the hotel and onto my journey to the peak. I had birthed questions during my reading, not doubts, but gaps in my understanding. I knew that the core of grace was faith, but my intellectual mind was grasping to rationalize. As I hiked up the ridge toward the top of the world, I tried to quiet my mind and let my heart fill with grace. As usual I found the universe conspiring to educate and deepen my faith. God is in the details, and the details were jumping out at me. I wondered, questioning omniscience, where was the beauty of creation when there was so much pain and inequality in the world. As I paused to catch my breath I looked down at the shards of rock at my feet. Previously I had only seen a barren landscape, but what I saw now made me drop to my knees. Every rock was covered with lichen of the most beautiful colors. In fact, the brownish color of the rocks was not the color of a mineral, but a rainbow of colors that blended at a distance. I looked at stone after stone and was filled with awe at the myriad shapes, as if some smith had desired to make each one a unique work of art. The communities that eked out an existence on the surface of each rock was infinitely complex. Dense, low, black and gray lichen grew, as if it was insinuating itself into the very lattice of the rock itself. Around, among, and on top of this race of flora grew multi-colored communities, some growing in smooth mounds like moss on a riverbank, and some approached a leafy shape like millions of entwining cabbages.

When I had my fill of eye-candy, I prepared to continue my ascent and placed the last rock I had been admiring back in its place. Looking down, I was stunned. My initial survey had found this land to be desolate and barren. But to see the beauty of creation we often have to quiet our minds and look closely and patiently. Growing through the rocks were the most magnificent and delicate flowers and grasses. Now I wasn't just on my knees, I brought my face to the ground in prostrate obeisance to the grandeur of the universe. In my mind a thought echoed—beauty is where we will look for it.

I pushed onward and upward, the midnight sun at my back, with newfound warmth and connectedness to this land I had first viewed as Godforsaken. Walking southward along the spine of this mountain the terrain dropped off quickly at my left, over the cliffs of the valley that held the town. On my right was a broad shoulder that stretched out to the ocean. Getting closer to the peak the shoulder narrowed, leaving me on a ridge above cliffs on one side and a sweeping bowl that spilled out to the sea on the other. I had been sheltered on the north side of the hill from a stiff breeze that hit me when I crested the ridge. The wind was coming from the southwest, bringing warm air from the Gulf Stream. I was at an elevation of thirty-five-hundred feet, heading toward the peak, which was forty-two-hundred feet above the rolling waves of the North Sea. The horizon line, from this altitude, would have been about three hundred miles or more, but visibility was limited to probably a hundred miles by the moisture in the air. From my vantage point I could see the entirety of a storm system with dark, foreboding clouds, riding the wind toward me. I could see the ragged edges of the storm nearest me and north and south. Only the back of the storm eluded my view. An hour later when I reached the peak, the storm was just striking the island and the sea boiled under its influence.

During my hike I had been repeating lines from the Bible and having a one-way discourse with the Creator that echoed into the deep reaches of my soul. Revelation of the beauty hidden in this barren landscape had turned up the volume of this discourse. I was having the conversation using words and images that, by their nature, are limited in their ability to describe the spiritual realm. I understood events described in the Bible and absorbed the words and images, but also felt the depth of expression that went deeper than words. Somehow the majesty of my environment ringing in my consciousness completed what language left unfulfilled.

I reached the peak and took in the three-hundred-and-sixty-degree view from the top of the world. The sun was low in the north, shining on the other side of the world, and its light cast a soft radiance on all that I looked upon. Looking back in the direction I had come, I saw the islands of Svalbard stretching to the north, with the sun sitting atop the peak of another island, like a star on a Christmas tree. To the west I saw the berg-choked ocean, and I shuddered, hoping that all the polar bears were happily hunting seals near the ice pack. The south and east were now shrouded by the storm. The clouds had settled about the island but my perch was cloud-free as the greedy fingers of the storm pushed over the lower ridges. The path I had taken was now obscured by clouds, and the moisture dissipated as it passed over the ridge. The town had clear skies and the tenants of the valley were unaware of the majestic power brewing just over the hill.

As I sat there, I heard rumblings of thunder and saw the tops of clouds lit up by lightning that was apparently striking the ground below. Looking down on the storm increased my feeling of sitting on top of the world, as only a few clouds were stacked higher than my vantage point. I sat meditating on the complexities of human intellect and the limitations of human thought in unraveling the great mystery. The sound of thunder rolled up the bowl and I felt the concussive waves wash over me. It was beautiful. The tops of the clouds were a phantasmagoric light show through which I could see the birth of lightning bolts. I began to get the strange feeling that my consciousness was somehow tied to the rhythm of the storm. It also seemed that there was a structure and cadence to the flashings and rumblings that manifested intelligibly just beyond my comprehension.

I thought of the tale of Mohamed meeting the angel Gabriel, who first appeared as a human. On Mohamed's insistence the celestial being revealed his true form, which filled the valley with fire and smoke of the terrifying angel.

Perhaps here on top of the world I was being given audience to put forth the shortcomings of my faith so that I might receive assurances. I thought that the lack of intelligibility might be due to the plethora of overlapping questions that danced in my head, bringing too many answers at one time. I quieted my spirit to focus on one aspect of grace to see if the rumblings might become coherent as my thoughts focused. I focused on the portrayal of, and roles assigned to, women in the doctrines of monotheistic beliefs. As my thoughts coalesced on the projected subservience of feminine energy in the dogma of Judeo-Christian tradition—Wham!—the loudest retort of thunder and the most brilliant flash of lightning occurred before me. The thrust of the shock waves was enough to flatten me against the ground as my mind reeled with the input of information. The dogma of male-dominated religions reinforced the fragile position of men vis-à-vis the holiness of women in relation to their connection to creation. The women are smarter. How did men end up with all the power? Religion played a large part once brute force became socially unacceptable. Wham, boom!

Religion should be a revolution of thought and a growing, evolving conceptual basis of understanding that should never become static. Yes, the world is round and revolves around the sun and zero is an important concept. With all the upheaval of dogma, why is the path to gender equality so long? The societal framework and archetypal understanding of a culture has a duty to march, courageously, toward truth, and the precepts important in one age are not necessarily so in another. How was the divine feminine being closed out of communal discourse? Wouldn't the world be a better place with greater balance? What social mores would have to get trampled, what social patterns would need transformational, not just incremental change?

The thought that rang in my brain was clear; it may or may not have made sense for the historical time period most of the Bible is set in, but it certainly isn't right now. Even the Bible reflects the evolution of human interaction in regards to women. More than forty biblical characters had multiple wives and while we are not sure of how common it was at the time, Deuteronomy does warn that a king should not have too many wives. And while there was never any acceptance of polyandry, the concept of polygyny was discouraged by Augustine and Luther and others and monogamy became codified in Judeo-Christian faiths over time. We need to figure out the next step and it may not come without a complete upheaval in the way we live, work, learn, etc.

As I regained my upright posture, I could see the storm forcing its way up the hill, threatening to overwhelm my position. Somehow, I knew that my line of questioning and my understanding of the response were active in keeping the storm at bay. One moment lacking clarity would lead me to being consumed by the blinding madness of the storm.

I held fast. Maintaining a lotus position at my station in the cosmos overlooking the planet, I humbly received truth. One assertion to the next was either bolstered or dashed against the pillars of God's throne. As the reciprocal interrogation continued, I led with inquiries of greater and greater complexity. I knew that this process needed to continue to completion even though I felt in grave danger of losing myself. The storm gathered its fury and I felt the awesome power rising up until it appeared that I was sitting on top of the clouds. I wanted to turn around and see, but even the break in concentration to wonder if the town was in clouds left the storm enveloping me further.

As I brought my attention back to this celestial discourse the clouds receded a little and I could once again see my legs. How long this went on before I passed out, I will never know.

The sun was to the south when I woke up from a deep slumber, cold and damp. I had been on the peak for twelve hours. How long I had slept, if it was sleep, I have no idea.

The clouds lay quietly below me as I wondered at the strange gift I had come to receive on my thirtieth birthday at the top of the world. I ate some of the food I had brought and gathered my strength. I took a route straight toward town that led down a ravine through the cliffs that overlooked the town. Unquestioned confidence assured me the way would be passable and safe.

Chapter Twenty One

Growing down. There is plenty of time in eternity for being gods; for now we are human and our heads should be with our bodies, present with our senses. It was a long way down from the mountain but I found myself back in the rhythm of what was quietly becoming my life.

During the holidays of 1995 we had sold two strains, one indica and one a potent sativa, named Excite and Yahoo, respectively. Apparently, Nathan was running the whisper play again. It didn't really click in my brain until the stories started coming out about the success of their initial public offerings. By the summer of '96 there was a Yahoo billboard on Houston and Lafayette that seemed to be advertising both the Web portal and the weed strain. Both were a huge success as Yahoo sold out before the summer was over.

With the harvest of 1996 we abandoned the whisper campaign and introduced Moonglow, which was actually a number of different strains in the same bag. The growers were producing so much quantity and amalgamating crops from other growers that it became an operational challenge to separate the strains. Interestingly, when you trim a number of strains from the same terroir (Cali sunshine, volcanic dirt, ocean mist) together and let them sit for a few weeks in pound bags, they blend together in terms of how they look and taste. There were differences in effect from bud to bud, depending on whether it was a sativa, indica or a blend. But from a marketing angle it worked to our advantage. If you smoke the same strain all the time you develop a resistance to its particular effects, but if you mix it up that doesn't happen. Most of the buyers didn't notice and just fell in love with the strain.

The real geeks started identifying different strains and

sharing feedback. I only heard this from a few friends to whom I sold ounces, as I was pretty distant from the retail side of things. There were a few connoisseurs who got mad about the lack of clarity about strains, but operationally there was no way for us to go back. We sold almost thirty thousand pounds per year of Moonglow in '97, '98 and '99, grossing well over $100 million per year.

I was chatting with Charlie Freedom during one of the first trips of the millennia and he added his two cents: "It takes some of the mystique away. We used to fly to Amsterdam and buy strains and come home and see which ones did best in our environment. There was a lot of competition in growing different strains and creating our own blends. I have a sativa-indica blend I call Cali Gold that was creating a name for itself; now it is all Moonglow with my other strains, and the strains of my neighbors. The only one I keep separate is the Haze, just because it looks so different. It is frustrating for me to see the beautiful plants with their unique qualities all tossed together and marketed under one brand. It mimics what is wrong with our consumer society. Ready-to-wear, off-the-shelf, monoculture agriculture, commoditizing products to satisfy the lowest common need instead of supplying benefits to customers that address their unique needs and taste."

"Keeping them separate would be a logistical nightmare."

"You will see. Someday soon websites will be selling strains with specific genetics aimed at specific users. I am sure they will include user comments and laboratory breakdowns as well."

"Weed on the Web?" I asked.

"It already is. AOL usergroups sell everything from sex and drugs to professional services. I was dating a girl whose login name was fuckmepumps and she was into all sorts of weird shit on AOL. There are a lot of twisted people enjoying the supposed anonymity of the internet."

"Is any of it anonymous?"

"Funny, I remember a conversation about 10 years ago when I still did a lot of trimming myself. There were some college kids from San Jose up here talking about the digital revolution for days on end. This was before any digital revolution had begun and I was pretty clueless to most of the debate. The one thing I came away with after that conversation is there won't be any privacy. Once personal information is ones and zeroes flying around, any number of players will be grabbing it to use to their own ends."

We were sitting in the booth where we always met and on a weekday afternoon the restaurant was empty. He took a few bites before wiping his lips and continuing.

"I guess we can only hope it will be used to sell us something. Like TV. If any actor or group was to have significant power and use it for the furthering of political interests we would really be in trouble."

It reminded me of what Garrett had said about how such information would be used and by whom. We finished our meal and got the truck loaded up.

"Can I give you a little advice before you go?"

"Of course, Professor."

"In short, I would say settle down. I don't think you can do that without getting out. I've known you a while now and the speed you are rolling at will take its toll. I am not saying move up into the mountains like I did, but there is an elegance in monotony that thrill-seekers miss while keeping their lives full of fireworks. Really, I am surprised you are as grounded as you are after the last ten plus years. When I first met you, I didn't think you would last a year. I am not saying I am seeing signs, but simple math says your tether is getting weak."

I opened my mouth to respond, but was silenced by Freedom's expression. He knew I was always at the ready with a quick rationalization from an intellectual point of view.

Realizing my answer would not have resonated with my truest self, I said nothing. After an awkward pause where he let the thought germinate, he gave me a hug and walked off.

I jumped in my rental car headed south to see Karen. It had been almost 10 years since we had met and our relationship was the most consistent thing in my life, beside airplanes, rental cars and hotels. Even my apartment in New York City felt like a hotel. Wilma, who cleaned the place and kept my plants alive, probably spent more time there than I did. Freedom was right, behind all the warrior-like bravado was the effect my lifestyle and my occupation was having on my psyche. Entering my fourth decade I was feeling a lot less punk and the sexiness of being a criminal was waning. Karen's house was becoming more like home for me than anywhere else. Not only was it a beautiful spot on the globe, but she was there.

I popped a tab at the start of the drive and by the time I got to Marin I was buzzing and the air was clear. Taking advantage of the good weather I hopped off the 101 and drove out to the headlands north of the Golden Gate Bridge. I grabbed a water bottle out of the car and walked toward the lighthouse. The lighthouse was closed and the steel door to the tunnel part of the trail would be locked. There is a spot where the land narrows and there is a little bridge straddling the ridge where in one direction was the Golden Gate and San Francisco and in the other was the open ocean. There was no one on the trail so I sat in the middle of the bridge with the great feats of humans standing proudly to one side and endless possibility if I turned my gaze to the other.

I was sitting in my own metaphor.

I understood the energy and excitement of dense populations and the great works this allowed. It ran in my blood. But I also knew it asked of most of us a heavy tribute in quality of life. While there was singing and dancing, along with them came flophouses and prostitution. While there was abundance for some, others were challenged. This complicated, messy affair was like the life I was living. It was bright and sparkly and free, but with it came a price I didn't often recognize. Freedom was prescient for sure.

As I looked to the ocean, I saw perfection and beauty in its vast uniformity. Unsullied by complicated structures and divisive dogma it was a blank canvas. Yet, while I don't believe in sea monsters even when tripping, I knew there were storms and winds and an obvious lack of hearth and home.

From the knitted brow of contemplation I was ripped open by the brilliant blaze psychedelics can provide, which tore me from my complex metaphor-building and left me laughing—laughing so hard it felt like I was crying. Then I was crying. Then laughing at myself crying, which made me laugh harder. When I got it together, I had to sacrifice my shirt to wipe my face of tears and snot. Having what felt like the first clear thought in years I realized, it wasn't complicated at all: I was living the life of a criminal. I was an active member of an ongoing illegal enterprise of massive proportions, no less. Somehow, I had successfully buried it under well-researched self-righteousness and familiarity of routine to the point where what I was doing felt normal. Running small trips from Arizona when I was younger seemed much riskier than what I was doing now, though the truth was quite the opposite.

Is it time to call it quits? Take Freedom's advice and slow down? How would I get out? What does that even feel like? Who am I?

The sun started to go down and the air chilled. My teeth were chattering when I got back to the car. Driving through the city at night was a perfect way to ride out the end of my trip. The trails of lights were like the thoughts in my head, brilliant sparks that faded and blurred into the background, leaving only whispers.

Karen wasn't home when I arrived at her place. I fell

asleep on her balcony hammock and woke up in the morning with a dew-covered blanket over me.

"Hey, sleepy head."

"Good morning, beautiful"

She looked at me differently. I saw concern I had never noticed before. Of course she recognized my energy shift; there was no hiding from her gaze.

"You okay?"

"Not sure where to start."

"We have plenty of time; let's start with breakfast."

Juice, squeezed from her trees, brought life back to my tired body. Karen giggled while she told me the story of her neighbor's troublesome goat that keeps getting in the house and has now eaten much of the furniture. That smile, her smile. It was common for me to feel as if I had spent a lifetime in a few hours with Karen, but now I was thinking past a few hours or a few days for the first time.

For the first time in my life I felt unsteady, unsure of how to proceed. I, who had always danced confidently into the unknown, was scared. I stumbled into the weed biz so early in my formative years that it was all I had known. Looking back I wondered if I had ever made a real decision in my life. Though all my actions and seized opportunities contributed to what looked like a choice, I never decided I wanted to be an outlaw. It had just happened. While it was uncomfortable for me to think of something beyond the life I had been living, it might just be time to actually make a choice in life.

There were plenty of other girls, but there was always Karen, even before I met her, as if she was created out of my imagination. I was terrified of giving the thought words out of fear of where they might lead.

"Where do you see yourself in 10 years?" I asked. I couldn't answer that question myself. I didn't know what I wanted.

"To be honest, I have been thinking lately about a

house with walls."

"Whoa, tipi girl in a house? You would probably hurt yourself on all those corners."

"It seems more settled; this is starting to feel like camping."

Every cell in my body was screaming to get on one knee and begin the eternity I hoped was waiting if I would just ask. Would she say yes? Why would she and yes to what? Marriage?

"You have been here a long time. Would you stay here?"

"Anyplace outside of an awesome city, close but also far from it, would work."

"Seems pretty good here," I added.

"It doesn't really matter where. But I will say there is weirdness here, like everywhere, but I tire of this particular kind of weirdness."

"Maybe we should do some traveling as research."

"We?"

"I would like to explore that."

"It seems to me we have had plenty of exploration, and I would love to travel with you. That said, I think we should change the topic before you get yourself in trouble."

"I like trouble."

There was a pause where the words and their meanings danced between us.

"All you have to do is ask."

That was it. She had made clear she would have me without me having to ask.

When I got back to New York I was in a daze. I couldn't plug into the energy I had loved so much. Sure, the city had changed over the course of the '90s. Freaks couldn't afford to live there anymore. Artists couldn't afford to live there anymore. There was a mass extinction of cool as the rents went up. Though the city had changed, I had changed more. It didn't have what I wanted; it didn't have Karen.

"You burnin' out," said Marteen. "You need a break; that's what's up. Come down to my place in Anguilla; a couple weeks on the beach make it irie."

"I am thinking about a bigger step back from the biz, but mostly I got girl trouble. I've been seeing a girl in Santa Cruz for more than ten years and now all of a sudden I got it bad."

"Been good for ten years, why change? You know what I think about long-term commitments."

"Yeah, long-term is a long weekend for you. I don't know, I am feeling like slowing down and building something instead of swinging like a player all the time."

"She dat good?"

"Yeah."

"Well, for the record, I say it would be a big mistake. I don't even know what it look like, a suburban home in a cul-de-sac? Kids? Soccer practices?"

"I know, I know, it sounds ludicrous to me too, but I have to admit I could use a different kind of normal for a while."

"What about the weed thing? I ain't ready to step off just yet."

"To be honest, I have no idea what I am doing, but I will make sure you are taken care of if I get out. And, you will come visit me on the cul-de-sac and meet my girl and my dog."

"You getting a dog?"

"Isn't that what you do? Get a dog, some kids, mow the lawn…" I paused before continuing, smiling at the irony. "Wow, I am fucked. That sounds really good to me. I mean, come on. I didn't like asparagus, but that changed. Life is change. I might be ready to try it."

"Be careful the picture you paint; you might be in it a long time."

"I think that is what scares me."

"Yeah, it should."

Marteen shared solid truth, but she is pretty far out there and probably not the best person to consult with about life. I knew what any sane person would say, but I had to hear it. I called my best friend from high school. I had seen Mike a few times over the decade and a half since school, and we got a call in at least once a year. Mike was one of the few people I really respected. He had dosed a few times and got it. He managed to party through college and rock the dean's list. He was married with three kids and earned plenty of money without giving up too much of his soul. He was doing it. I acted like I didn't want that life, but truthfully, I couldn't do it. I hadn't learned to embrace life at a lower volume.

We spoke for a while about his journey to parenting. It seemed like he was doing a better job than most of the fathers we had known growing up.

"Anyone who says they are a good parent is crazy. You might get lucky and have a good fit, but they are their own assholes. One of my kids is a piece of cake. He learns the way I can teach, trusts me when I tell him he is about to get hurt, has a short emotional recovery time and the other two have been an intense learning lesson."

"That sounds like a lot of work."

"I am trying to find beauty in a life of service."

"How is that working out?"

"Most of the time pretty good, but there have been plenty of times I am glad there was no video rolling."

Mike ordered another round and asked, "So what did you want to talk about?"

"I need some advice, but in order to get that advice I have to tell you a story that I can't tell anyone. I am going to tell you and you are going to forget you ever heard it."

I could have kept it simple: 'I sell a lot of weed,' but after a dozen years of living like an undercover spy I wanted to share it with somebody. Mike was a perfect candidate.

"Holy shit, dude. It is like one of the conspiracies we talked about in school, but you are in it. Holy shit. I bought all those strains and Moonglow has been my steady for a few years. Holy shit, that was you?"

I let it sink in before I asked him what he thought.

"Well, let's start with the obvious. What the fuck are you doing? Get out. It sounds like you had some good luck, but it can't last forever. I don't understand how you can sleep at night. I drive with a quarter-ounce and I am nervous."

"Somehow it became normal."

"You don't seem crazy besides all the evidence you shared to the contrary."

"I am starting to feel a little crazy."

"Yeah, dude, you had a good run. Time to move on."

"And what about the girl thing? Do you enjoy being married? You know me, can I do it?"

"Well, that is tougher. Is marriage all bliss? Certainly not. Is it worth it? It has been for me. There are plenty of challenges because they are smarter, and crazier than we are. I say if you have known her for so long, you probably won't get a better chance to give it a try. Is there anything keeping you from getting out?"

"Fear of boredom. Also my own mythology is thick with an outlaw theme. Do outlaws have kids? Normal lives? What kind of outlaw doesn't break the law?"

"I am sure you will continue to break the speed limit," Mike said, making us both crack up.

It helped. Finally telling somebody the truth made it feel like less of a burden. Six months earlier I didn't even recognize the burden. I was so engrossed in the romance adventure story I was busy crafting there was no room for rational thoughts about the risks.

Chapter Twenty Two

I arrived in the Golden Triangle in March of 2000, thinking I was going to pick up a load as usual. I tripped down nostalgia lane as I turned off the freeway. My first trip out was 1983 to trim and the beauty of the region still moved me the same way as when I was a teenager. The Golden State had become part of who I was. From the fashion fiends of L.A. to the freaks of San Fran and the farmers of Humboldt it was as familiar to me as my hometown. At center, both geographically and mentally, was a tipi in Trout Gulch.

I pulled up to the restaurant and was surprised to see the parking lot full of cars. When I walked through the door, I realized it was a reunion. Rose, Nathan and even Garrett were there. A couple of growers I knew and some people I didn't know were already seated and I was told we were waiting for a few stragglers. Big Jim and Freedom sat next to me when they arrived and Robert joined us. At some point it was decided everyone was there and the door was locked, staff sent home and we had a proper party. Though few of us actually knew everyone, it was surely a gathering of like-minded individuals. No one asked about what part was played by whom, but we knew everyone in the room had played a part.

After an hour or so, Nathan gathered our attention. "I wanted you all here so you can hear this at the same time so there won't be any miscommunications. We are done. This fellowship has fulfilled its role and it is time to disband."

A murmur went through the room before Nathan continued, "I invited you here so we can have a bit of ceremony and break bread while talking joyously about something none of us will ever speak of again." He looked around the room to be sure we all understood his meaning.

“It has been an honor working with you on this project, newcomers and old friends alike, and I want to share my gratitude to each of you for the commitment we showed to each other in keeping this secret for so long. There are a few important points I want to share, first about why now and second about what now.

“New federal banking regulations and oversight are becoming more challenging to overcome and frankly I never thought this would go as long or be as successful. There is also renewed pressure to legalize marijuana and some of that conversation is louder than our project, especially considering the computing vertical doesn’t need our support anymore. Finally, and I tell you this because it is a good story, Banjo had a run-in with a now famous goombah who was actually a federal informant that left some lingering files we can’t control much longer. Ask him about that one.

“Finally, what now? Most importantly, diversify right away. We don’t know how much our efforts have contributed to this bubble, but once the spigot is off there will certainly be some effects in the market. Call your brokers tomorrow. We brought cash to pay for this last load and once we liquidate this last trip, all operations will be shut down.

“Now I want to let Garrett say a few words. Some of you don’t know but Garrett had a bit of a think tank supported by our efforts that has done a tremendous amount to shape the development of the Web in as democratic a way as possible. Garrett, the floor is yours.”

“As this whole episode was so compartmentalized, many of you may not know of the political, legal and philosophical debates our efforts helped to shape. Over the years some of the money from this adventure has been funneled into efforts to influence the development of the web. I have some information on the table to share that can’t leave this room that brags a bit of our exploits, both public and clandestine. My concern is while one part of the battle is won, keeping the

Web from being dominated by commercial or political forces is a fight that will continue. All our efforts had been supported by the New York City retail operation and that will be ceasing operations. So I have chosen tonight to announce the existence of a not-for-profit to continue our efforts. I hope you will all consider making sizable contributions."

Nathan, surprised by Garret's brevity, broke the ensuing silence, "Let us celebrate".

I was nursing a pint and not in a rush to eat when Big Jim and Freedom came to my table with stacked plates.

"So Banjo, what now?" asked Big Jim.

"I don't know. I have been considering getting out for a while now. It has just been too easy and lucrative to quit and I haven't come up with a 'what next' yet. Maybe I should become a grower like you guys."

"I would say the glory days of the grower are over. Too many people in the game and too many of them are knuckleheads. I would recommend insurance," said Freedom

"Insurance?"

"What other product does no harm and makes people feel better?"

"Wow, Professor, that was a stretch, but I get your point. I am thinking a little middle of the road might be good for a decade or two. As sexy as all this has been, I think I am ready to try something else."

I really didn't know what was next. I always knew it would end, but hadn't thought it through. In an attempt to get the spotlight off me I asked, "What about you guys? Surely you don't need to grow anymore."

"Both Freedom and I have rented our land to others to break their backs on and for a few years now have mainly been acting as brokers."

"Well, if that doesn't pop the bubble. I thought you guys love to grow."

"Of course, we are still growing, but 10 or 20 plants is a

hobby. When you get into the hundreds there is no way around it; it is work and we don't need to work anymore," Freedom said with a smile.

We all toasted to that truth as Robert rejoined our table, and after a second toast Freedom and Jim left to mingle.

"Didn't see this coming," Robert said, though he probably understood better than most of us why the regulatory challenges were becoming a factor. "I guess I don't have to stay in Sacramento anymore. Jeez, is it time to settle down?"

"Seems to me you were pretty settled."

"I never liked Sacramento, that is why I never looked for a serious romance. I really didn't think I would end up there so long."

"Life is what happens," I added.

Robert turned to look me in the eye, but I stopped him before I endured another person asking me what was next.

"I don't know what it looks like or where it is, but if all these years of LSD experiences have taught me anything it is we are here to grow down. I have spent years dancing with the gods and angels but we are only here for a short time and there is plenty of time in eternity to be celestial."

"Are you tripping now?"

I couldn't answer right away. I hadn't imbibed, but I felt spiritually weightless, like the first rush of a trip.

"No, but I feel a bit rudderless. I appreciate the kick in the ass to get out of the business, but now I am faced with a question I can't answer."

"It is all about love," Robert said, "Keep true to your heart and you will be fine."

"What about you? Are you going to stay in banking?"

"I have been thinking about buying a boat to take people ocean fishing."

"I didn't know you like fishing."

"I don't know if I do, or boats or ocean for that matter. I just want to live a different life for a while. Or maybe a horse ranch, but I have never met a horse. I feel like this is an opportunity to try something different. Most people only get to live one life, maybe we can squeeze in two."

The night wore on with the telling and retelling of individual adventures, close calls and awkward moments. I laughed a lot and enjoyed the party, but wasn't really present as my subconscious was on overdrive. As I got ready to leave I realized one thing, a business card was never going to define me and life has to be about the other stuff.

After the shindig, I drove straight to Karen.